MICAH

REBECCA ROYCE

Printed in the United States of America

First Printing, 2018

Paperback ISBN: 978-1-947672-42-0

Ebook ISBN: 978-1-947672-21-5

Cover Artist: AG Covers

www.rebeccaroyce.com

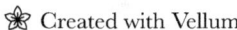 Created with Vellum

Dear Reader

Dearest Reader,

Thank you so much for picking up Micah. If you are reading this (and thank you so much for doing so!), I am going to assume you have met Micah already in one of the other six books where he plays a secondary role. (Those books could be Initiation, Driven, Subversive, Redemption, Justice, and Deacon. The first five are from my Young Adult series, The Warrior, and Deacon is from the New Adult spin-off, Warrior World.)

Micah has always been a favorite for me and for the readers. I am so happy to finally be able to give Micah his own voice and the chance to tell his story. The truth is, we only think we know him. I hope you are as surprised by Micah Lyons as I was.

If you don't receive my newsletter, please pop over to www.rebeccaroyce.com and sign up. I'd love to stay in touch.

Hugs,
  Rebecca Royce

...

My name is Micah Lyons, and I was told, not so much asked, to write down my thoughts for posterity. My writing something down that others will read falls into the sort of funny category, considering what a bad writer I am. I was never really up for school. Not in the time before this one, and not now.

I'd much rather be doing things than thinking about doing them or talking about doing them. Give me a task, I get the shit done. I see the Vampires in the distance, roaming the night, seeking blood, hunting and killing us. Then I remember what we all learned—they're really people who are sick. Some of them can be saved.

But fixing things doesn't fall into my purview. Sick people who suck blood are not my problem. I'm a Warrior. It's not my job to save them. It's my job to kill them. From now until whenever one of them kills me.

See? I told you, people who are reading this, I'm not any good at writing.

Chapter 1

The afternoon sun forced me awake when what I really wanted to do was spend at least six more hours asleep. Getting up during the daytime when I was in Genesis was pointless for me. Between the sun's hard assault on my eyelids and the girl snoring next to me—reminding me I wasn't alone—it was time to get up and get moving.

I sat up, cracking my neck and stretching my arms over my head. Twenty-two years old, and my body was so beat up I woke every morning stiff like I was ninety. I rubbed my eyes. Who was I kidding? No one lived to be ninety. Stiff like I was forty. Four decades was the best I could hope for, probably.

"Matthew"—the girl next to me rolled over, touching my hip—"lie back down. Let's sleep and then go at it again."

Last night, I hadn't minded how she called me *Matthew*, which wasn't even close to my name. Forgetting I was responsible for saving her life and she should really know my first name, I'd wanted to get lost inside someone so badly, I hadn't bothered to correct her. Embarrassing a girl by correcting her was a sure way to ensure she wouldn't spread her legs for me. The goal was to be inside her pussy. If she wanted me to be Matthew, I'd be Matthew.

Apparently, Micah was too hard to remember.

I didn't even remember our actual joining, which was okay because she didn't know my name. It wasn't like she could go around telling everyone if I'd been less than satisfactory under the sheets. The poor Matthew fellow she could go right ahead and complain about.

"Sorry, sweetheart." Okay, maybe I didn't know her name either. "I've got things to do today." I swung my legs over the side of the bed. "Make sure you go down and register in the office. All you newbies have to be assigned jobs."

She groaned and rolled over. Only two days earlier, she'd been in a Vampire cage with five others when I'd walked into the facility and freed them. It had taken us 48 hours to get back here. Lately, I'd been the one-man welcoming committee to Genesis. Not that I complained. I didn't want company on my explorations.

It was better to do these things alone.

There were few people I could tolerate for long periods of time, and all of those people had gotten married, which made them unavailable to get lost in Vampire lairs with me.

My own company was fine.

The last piece of clothing I located was my green hoodie. I'd stolen it off a Vampire before I dusted him. When the vamps died, the stuff they had on went with them. The whole thing was so bizarre. I'd washed and washed the piece of attire until I was sure it was clean, and now I wore it all the time. For autumn weather, it was perfect. Particularly when I constantly went in and out of

Vampire lairs, which were hot. It was hot, then it was cooler. Hot. Cooler. Hot. Cooler.

The hoodie let me layer. I might have been slightly obsessed with the thing. It was the first article of clothing I'd acquired for myself since waking up in this strange version of existence. Everything else had come from Genesis and been handed to me.

I was a little bit proud of my hoodie.

Leaving the girl's tent, I stared at the sky. It was going to rain. Time to head out or get caught in weather that soaked me to the bone. I had ground to cover. Every time I found more people and rescued them from monsters, I had to bring them back here, which I was happy to do. But I'd have to backtrack. Again and again and again. I needed to know how far the underground system went and where the scientists who controlled the Vamps were.

"Micah Lyons." The call from Deacon Evans halted my progress.

He was my best friend. I didn't know which of us was more surprised by our relationship, but there it was.

"Deacon Evans," I spun and walked backward. "Wife pregnant yet?"

Deacon rolled his eyes. "No. Did you knock anybody up I should be concerned with?"

"I don't know if it should concern *you*." I held out my hands in front of me to ward him off if he decided to punch me. Bantering with him was fun, and I smiled, maybe for the first time in weeks. "No, no one is pregnant."

I always suited up, and since sex no longer seemed to take the edge off, I was probably going to start cutting down how much I indulged. Wow. When had I gotten so fucking old?

"Where are you off to?" When he caught up to me, I turned once more, and we headed toward my tent.

"Back down."

Deacon sighed. "Already? You've been here a whole 24 hours. I wouldn't even have seen you if I hadn't bumped into you now."

It was sort of *convenient* he had. "Aw, Deacon. Are you missing me so much you're stalking me?"

The comment earned me a punch on the arm, and I laughed. If every day could be like this, maybe I would stick around. But I knew better. Genesis didn't mean only good times with Deacon Evans. It meant family obligations, disapproving stares, and the constant knowledge I disappointed my parents every time I opened my mouth. Remaining meant no self-determination.

I was between a rock and a hard place. I needed Genesis. I'd never survive leaving entirely. But staying meant being trapped under rules I had no say in, surrounded by the same people day in and day out.

I had to keep living this in between life.

Deacon sighed. "I do miss you. Asshole."

I snorted. "Sorry. I'll be back. A couple of weeks, if not sooner."

My friend looked up at the sky. "Shit, it's going to rain. If you're going, you should go—unless you want to stay. That's an option, too."

"Was just going to swing by my tent and go from there." We'd practically reached my designated area, and I'd hardly noticed the time pass. The Warriors were all housed together in shelters originally designed for us by Dr. Icahn, the madman who destroyed our lives to begin with. The little living quarters were more like collapsible permanent homes. Our engineers had hooked us up basic plumbing, which would make actually collapsing them a problem now. There was talk about building actual houses, but so far, the plan was only talk.

Despite the fact I didn't currently perform Warrior duties, they hadn't kicked me out of my spot and into general housing yet. Our tents were slightly bigger. Not that I was in mine enough for it to matter. Still, this had been mine since we moved above ground. I didn't want to live somewhere else when I had to be here.

Deacon jerked his chin toward the hills behind us. "Be careful out there. Lots and lots of Vampire activity at night in those hills. It's like they're looking for something."

I was, too. Maybe I had something in common with the bloodsuckers. Only, I had no idea what I searched for anymore.

I spent an hour swapping clothes. Although I took the hoodie with me everywhere, I did alter the shirts I wore underneath. I needed underwear. Pants. Socks. Food. Water. A first aid kit. Condoms. My ink and needles.

The last bit I probably wouldn't use, since I didn't ink my own skin and I traveled alone. Still, I brought them every time. If pressed, I wasn't sure I could say why I did it. Not that anyone ever asked. Outside of Deacon, most people gave me a wide berth. Well, save for my family. They tended to get in my face as much as he did. Probably wise on the part of everyone else.

I walked out of Genesis without incident. The civilians weren't allowed beyond a certain point. The rules were simple. For everyone's safety, only the Warriors could come and go. But not even the Warriors could exit the way I did.

I'd pushed against the boundaries until the powers that be—also known as my father— bent them for me. Even then, I'd only gotten so much space because of my last name. It pissed me off that they treated me differently, but it didn't prevent me from taking advantage of the privilege. I would lose my mind if I had to stay here.

I sighed. *Enough.*

With the sun in the sky, I wasn't afraid of the Vampires, and I trudged up into the hills without a backward glance. Instead, I kept my gaze toward the clouds. I'd always loved the world above our heads.

As a child, in the Before Time, I'd been a daydreamer. Eventually, that title had changed to inattentive. Ultimately, the titles had been something akin to loser and disappointment. At one point, my father had suggested I wasn't worth the air I got to breathe for free. That had been a really *super* day. But then we'd all been frozen and woken up here. So, what did it matter, really?

I climbed down into the Vampire hole with the distinction of having been so active Vampires had poured out of it to kill us—or to tried to—every night. Now it was relatively empty. I hadn't run into a Vampire in weeks in this part of the underground maze.

Deacon said they'd been having a lot of action… so where were they coming from?

I'd see if I could figure it out. Much as I wanted long breaks from my family and friends, I didn't want them dead or injured. I helped when I could.

The ladder was rickety. If I kept doing this, I would have to replace it at some point. Next time I came through, I would bring tools. Fluorescent lights blinked on and off when I reached the bottom. They could probably use a change, but I was fresh out of those types of light bulbs. They'd not made it to this new existence with us. Although, it seemed the Vampires and the crazy scientists who controlled them with addiction probably had some.

I'd find out.

And just the idea I was going to have to start repairing

these places was fucking ridiculous. I smirked. That was life. Or whatever. I wasn't a ninety-year-old man reflecting on shit. I was exploring Vampire holdings and saving people's lives.

There wasn't anything better for me to do.

I'd no sooner rounded a corner when my senses went into overdrive, causing my head to violently spin. I doubled over, grabbing on to my knees. Memory washed over me, bringing dizziness in its wake.

"What are we going to do about Micah?" My mother sighed. She set her coffee on the table and palmed her eye.

My father shook his head. "Do about him? What do you suppose we should do? He's lazy, and he's pretty much a player."

My parents hadn't known I was there, or they'd not have said those things. The fact that they spoke without knowing I was there didn't mean I shouldn't have heard what they said. I wasn't even surprised. They sat around the kitchen table at night, and they talked. They always had. On nights my father came home in time to have this kind of conversation, they discussed all of us.

I was one of five children, and we were the only family in town with so many children-slash-siblings running around. It was trendy to have three, and most people had two. My parents had always done things their own way and damn the consequences. They were stricter on us than any other family around, too. Yes, ma'am. No, sir. Nowhere in our small New Jersey town did I hear that kind of talk except inside our own walls.

My father was an FBI agent, a pretty important one. I supposed I should know more than *important* about his position, but I didn't because I didn't care. He was a big time hero. Yeah. Yeah. Yeah. We could only afford to live where we did in this town where everyone was richer than us because my mother's father had left us the house. The taxes were in some kind of low bracket thanks to a deal Grandpa had once made with the county. They thought I didn't know that shit. Maybe my siblings didn't. I did.

I heard things I shouldn't when no one knew I listened.

"He's not Chad." My mother sighed again. She was doing that a lot lately when it came to me. "We can't count on him getting a scholarship from the Icahns."

My father shook his head. "No, he's certainly not Chad."

"Patrick." Admonishment filled her voice, but not as much as I might have hoped. "Micah is sweet."

"I'm pretty sure he's having sex with half the student body."

It wasn't quite so many as he said. I closed my eyes. No, I wasn't my big brother, Chad, the perfect son. I loved him or I'd hate him. Next they'd bring up Tia, the only girl and a year younger than me. She really could do no wrong. Then my younger brothers were pretty much babies and unsullied by choices.

I slammed the outside door to get out of hearing their diatribe about my flaws. Maybe I should sleep with everyone in the class. My parents both shut up. I might not be as smart as the rest of my family, but I was the only one who knew how to be quiet, and a general knowledge on how to go through life without everyone knowing where you were all the time had to count for something.

Hurt made me want to lash out, but instead, I didn't say a word. What was the point? They thought I was an idiot, and they were probably right.

"Hey." I stepped into the dining room far enough to lean against the door. "How's it going tonight?"

Then, I was thrust back into the here and now, away

from my memory of a time I'd never return to and was better left unvisited in my own head.

"*What. In. The. Ever. Loving. Fuck?*"

A deep but feminine voice answered me. "I'm sorry. That happens when I'm around sometimes."

I raised my head to look out through the blinking lights. They were going to give me a headache if I didn't get out of this section soon. I knew whose voice I heard. Truth was, I'd been wondering if I would run into her since I learned who she was.

The lunatic scientists who inflicted this special hell on the world had managed to, after having themselves cloned lots of times, turn one Vampire back. To cure her of the virus which had made her a Vampire to begin with. Out of thousands they'd tried to fix, she was the only one who had gotten better.

Then she'd managed to escape captivity with the help of one of the scientists who now lived at Genesis. We'd all been briefed on the former Vampire named Brynna. She brought memories with her when she arrived places, caused the other people to suddenly get lost in their own minds. We had no idea why.

And that was certainly what had happened.

She was dark haired, a stark contrast to the flashing light in the room with us. "Brynna, right?"

I phrased it as a question when it wasn't one. Sounded somehow more polite.

"Micah, yes?"

Seemed she was doing the same thing. I pointed up at the light. "Can we do this somewhere other than this headache inducing flashing light fest?"

Normally, I could be charming. I hated the constant blinking light. She looked to where I pointed and then back to me. "Sure, follow me. If you want."

There was a challenge in how she phrased her invitation. Or maybe it was her tone. I didn't know. Did she think I wouldn't follow her because she'd been a fanged, blood-sucking monster and now she was something else? Well, she'd soon see I didn't scare easily.

Monsters were basically what I did. She was another in a long line.

I followed her along the blinking hallway until we ended up in a room where the lights were solid. Fluorescent, yes, but at least they were steady.

I took a better look at her. Brynna's long, dark hair fell past her waist in waves. Her face was long. She had a small cleft in her chin and high cheekbones. Her eyes were pixie like, and her nose Grecian. She was lovely. When Deacon had described her, he hadn't said she was so pretty. But then again, my best friend really only had eyes for his wife.

The woman in front of me was of medium build. Her height or weight wouldn't have mattered when she was a Vampire. They were deadly in all sizes. The child Vampires, which were the worst to see, had taken down full grown men.

She put her hands on her hips. "Are you done?"

"I've never seen a former Vampire before. You'll have to excuse me, I wanted a good look." I smirked at her. "And you're actually pretty to view. Might have taken my time."

The woman snorted. "Does that work for you? Your handsome face and your quick tongue? Do women fall to the floor and beg Micah Lyons, one of the unofficial crown princes of Genesis, to please take their pants off them?"

I laughed. It was a hard sound, the need for the burst of amusement surprising me the second it happened. "None have actually said, 'Take my pants off me, Micah.' "

"You get the point." She spun in a circle. "I look like a human."

She did, indeed. "How did you know my name?"

"I know lots of things."

Well, if that was going to be the only answer I got, then I supposed it would do. She hadn't inquired as to why I knew who she was, which wasn't surprising. If she knew me, then she was also aware we'd learned of her existence. Deacon really needed to be more forthcoming when it came to his interactions with others and what was said.

"I suppose this saves us the trouble of having to introduce ourselves."

She tilted her head to the side. "I suppose. What are you doing down here? Time after time by yourself? Are you trying to get killed? To get turned?"

"Hard to turn a Warrior."

Brynna nodded. "Hard but not impossible. I turned one or two in my time. I'll ask again, Warrior, what are you doing down here alone?"

"None of your business, Vamp Girl."

Her dark brown eyes flared hot for a second, and then she masked her face again. "It is my business. I can't be expected to keep an eye on the scientists and watch out for you."

"If I needed to be watched, I suppose that would be true, but seeing as I neither want nor need your help, you can go back to whatever it is you think you're doing down here."

She held up three fingers on her right hand. "That's how many times I have stopped you from dying and you had no idea. I'm getting a little tired of doing it."

Saved me? Bullshit. "When?"

"You didn't even know. You make my point for me. When you went after those humans in the cage, who I was in the process of getting out, there was a horde of Vampires headed straight for you. I waylaid them, and they didn't get to you in time. Another time, there were Werewolves, and the last time, you almost walked into a trap and I got rid of the trap first."

I had seen relatively few Vampires lately, no Werewolves, and I really had no idea about any traps. "Thank you. You can stop now. I don't need or want your help."

I really didn't. I was supposed to be doing this alone, and it turned out I'd had someone cleaning up for me? Her fixing things negated the whole point. If I was overwhelmed and killed down here, then so be it.

"Micah." She raised her voice. "You have a life up there. You're a *Lyons*." I was fully aware, and hearing her say it did not endear her to me, at all. "Go back to it. I'm clearing out these places. I'll get the humans free. I don't have time for spoiled, entitled, so-called Warriors coming down here and mucking things up."

I'd been called many things in my life. Spoiled and entitled had never been one of them. I couldn't let those accusations stand. I walked toward her, slowly. We really didn't know anything about this woman—creature—whatever she was. All we knew was she'd been cured of her Vampirism. She was clearly not entirely human. If she were, we wouldn't be overwhelmed with memories every time she came near.

She was something different, that was for sure. I'd learned, night after night, hour after hour, that in the end, monsters always wanted us dead. She claimed to have saved me. Well, how nice of her. I still wasn't going to take her shit.

When I was close enough to tell she smelled like soap and fresh air, I stopped. "I don't hurt women. Not ever. Human ones, anyway. And to be clear, most women I know could probably kick my ass if they wanted. But I don't know what you are, and I don't take insults from monsters." She winced, and I immediately regretted the statement. Didn't stop me from continuing. In for a penny, in for a pound. "I'm not any of the things you say I am. I'm down here to search the place, rescue people, and report back. If I die doing it, then at least it was doing something to save the people of Genesis. If you want the Genesis life so much, the one you accused me of leaving, go grab it for yourself. Oh wait... you can't, right? Because you're a Vampire. Cured or not. You killed however many people you did. And now you're stuck here in the dark. Forever."

I'd never seen anyone move as fast as Brynna did. One second she was in front of me, and the next she was gone.

I breathed in through my nose. Okay, she'd triggered me, and I was a huge asshole. I'd own it. Spoiled and entitled? No.

Dick? Yes.

Chapter 2

As the day went on, my treatment of the beautiful Vampire girl continued to bother me. That was quite the oxymoron. Beautiful. Vampire. The two terms shouldn't go together. And yet, they did. Brynna was gorgeous and for most of the last who-knew-how-many years had been a blood-sucker. How were both possible?

I already knew I was stupid, but I couldn't seem to reconcile the two together. I sighed. She'd struck at my ego, and I'd hit back. At some point, I had to stop being such an asshat and quit responding before I had the chance to think about what I was going to say. Not every attack by me—verbal or physical—had to be fatal.

I rounded the corner and stopped. The hairs on the back of my neck stood up. Something was wrong. I grabbed the stake out of my hoodie pocket and was ready to fight if need be. We'd been taught to trust our gut in fights. My body felt cold. That was a Vampire sign. Were-wolves were pain.

When I'd been messed with during cryogenic sleep, those warnings were implanted inside of me so I could always tell when a Vampire was near. Funny, I'd not felt anything like the signal when Brynna was near. Just memories of Mom and Dad discussing what a bitter disappointment I'd been. Not a Vampire signal the entire time.

I stepped forward, and a hand reached out from the darkness to cover my mouth.

"Don't bite me," Brynna spoke in a low whisper. "And don't make a frickin' sound."

I nodded. Biting the Vampire would be quite a role reversal. I didn't intend to give it a go. I remained still, and she eventually released my mouth.

I listened to the sounds around me and tried to ignore the fact that Brynna smelled good and was pressed against me. I wasn't a sex addict, at least I didn't think I was, and this was clearly not the moment to be thinking about anything other than what was happening. I'd gone through years of training, and it was like I'd lost all of it in the hours I'd been down here.

I blamed Brynna.

Voices traveled toward us, and she tugged on my arm, drawing me farther into the dark. The little woman put her body in front of mine in the shadows. What in the hell was she doing? I grabbed her. I didn't need her to stand in front of me, but she kicked my shin and as I digested that she could actually wield a lot of pain with her small foot, a noise nearby forced me into silence. The cold Vampire feeling shot through my body.

Out of the doorway I'd been about to enter, two scientists strode forward. They spoke to each other and didn't look up to see us. One was a tall, older woman with salt and pepper hair, and the other was a man about the same age. He was totally bald.

"I mean look at the amino acids. What we really need is Icahn. I think it's time to bring him back."

I jolted, and Brynna's fingers dug into my arm. Okay, I'd stay silent. Behind the scientists, two Vampires seemed to float, rather than walk, after them. The Vampires didn't attack the scientists. They were addicted to a substance the scientists kept in their human food supply. I guessed it didn't make sense to bite the hand feeding them...

Then again, maybe they had stronger cognition than that. The woman in front of me was perfectly able to speak. Had she gotten the ability back or had she never lost it?

The taller of the two Vampires turned slightly in our direction. I gripped the stake in my hand. Okay, if it was go time, then it was go time. I'd...

His gaze fell to Brynna and, for a second time, seemed to slow down. Images blew through my consciousness. Scenes from my life I never thought about. The time my father had taken Chad and me to see the Yankees play. We'd had nosebleed tickets. They'd lost, but it had been fun. Chad and I had thrown popcorn at each other, and my Dad had actually laughed for a change.

The memory faded fast, the Vampires looking away from us as they continued following the scientists. Brynna let out the breath she must have been holding. The room finally cleared.

"What the fuck?" I still kept my voice low.

Brynna turned to look at me. "Two scientists and the Vampires they keep in tow."

"No, *that* I got." I rolled my eyes. "The memory. Why does it keep happening around you?"

She sucked in a breath. "You felt that? A memory? When Ivan looked at us."

"I..." I swallowed through the dryness in my throat. "The Vampire has a name?"

Brynna left me and headed toward the now vacant

room. "Of course he had a name. We all have names. I believe we've already done introductions, you and I."

I sighed and hastened to follow. Our second meeting was not going better than our first. "Yes, I know you have a name. Did you have one when you were…"

"A monster?" she interrupted.

The room we entered was large. I'd seen ones like it before. It seemed every time I came down into these hell-holes, I found more and more spots I'd missed. Was it ever going to be possible to map all of it? I couldn't waste time doing this. I'd just been given an incredible piece of information. They were going to re-clone Isaac Icahn. His return would be a nightmare I couldn't allow.

Yet still, I followed Brynna further into the testing room. That's how I thought of these places anyway. Like the others I'd explored, the place was thrown around as though it had been vacated quickly. Beakers, vials, and pieces of microscopes were all over the floor. I bent over and picked one up.

I still had yet to answer Brynna. She'd used the M word in an obvious reference to the fact that earlier I'd used it to describe her. I could continue this fight—maybe die on this hill, as the expression went—or actually not be a jackass.

"I'm sorry I called you a monster." I couldn't help the smirk on my mouth as I continued. "You're a reformed monster. Big difference. A recovering monster."

She groaned. "I keep saving your life, and you keep being…" She motioned toward me with her hand. "This person."

"Why do you keep doing it then?" I squatted down, rummaging through the broken glass to see if there was anything there worth saving. Or maybe it was simply to find something to do with my hands.

"Hasn't there been enough death?" She looked away

from me. "To answer your earlier question, Ivan recognized me as I did him. The memories… they're a result of whatever they did to cure me of my Vampire disease. Vampires live in each other's memories all the time. It's what we do. You're being pulled into it with me for the brief seconds you're in my presence."

I got to my feet. All of this was different from anything I understood about the bloodsuckers. "What?"

"Which part didn't you understand?" She kicked a table. "It's not here. I was sure it would be since they kept it hidden so long. I bet it's on Dr. Marco. I don't want to kill her. Go home, Micah. I think you heard some information you're going to want to get to your father. Stay out of my Vampire maze. Today's the last time I'll ever be saving your life."

I didn't know what I would have said to her. Between the understandable jab and her ordering me out of the Vampire lairs, I stood there with my mouth open while she ran away, disappearing too fast for me to follow her. Again.

I sighed. Today was not going how it was supposed to. Not even a little bit. What made it worse was she was correct. I did have to go back and tell them about Icahn. My need to keep exploring was going to have to wait another day. Again. Maybe I was fooling myself. Maybe I would never get out of Genesis. Maybe I should quit trying.

Only, giving up had never been in my nature. I wasn't done yet. And if the fascinating woman—monster—*whatever*—thought she could order me around, she had another think coming.

FINDING my father wasn't a problem. Patrick Lyons ran

Genesis with a sometimes soft, sometimes iron, fist. Sometimes he was gentle, and sometimes he was so hard he could smash through rock. I always got the iron part of him. Dad spent most of his time these days sitting behind a table, giving orders to anyone foolish enough to be in his vicinity when he felt like dishing them out. Or worked for him. Whatever the case happened to be.

I rushed into the room to see a line of people waiting to speak to him. Family relations aside, I would normally stand patiently for an audience with the old man. It wasn't like we enjoyed speaking to each other.

But this had to take precedence.

"Hey," I shouted, waving my hands in the air. "Dad, I need your attention. Now."

He raised his eyes to meet my gaze and then nodded. It was probably the now that got his attention. He had to know how little I wanted his immediate attention on anything I did. Or didn't do.

When the room cleared, my father got to his feet. "What's going on? I thought you had gone again. Didn't even stop by to see your mother."

Guilt pressed against my temple like the nasty bitch that emotion always proved to be, and I shoved it away. I didn't have time for emotional battering. "I was gone. I came back because I learned something, and you need to hear it, too."

"Go on." My dad put both his hands on the table in front of him, leaning forward. "It's bad."

Maybe it was my tone that tipped him off. "Two scientists running around down there talked about re-cloning Icahn. They need him for something. They're going to bring him back."

I expected dad to burst into action. Immediate response was his way. He'd charge to the door and start barking orders. Only, he didn't. Instead, my father sank in his chair. He was forty-seven years old. Fit, healthy, and larger than life was how I'd always thought of him. Suddenly, worry for his health had me charge to the table.

"Are you okay?"

He waved his hand at me. "I'm not having a heart attack."

Okay, well that was that. My father rubbed his eyes. "This is what we feared. How to get all the cloning machines. It's impossible. Tiffani and I talked about this many times. The idea he could be back."

I hadn't known. I supposed I should have considered it. But once Icahn was dead, thrown over the edge of a balcony by the now deceased Werewolf, Andon Kenwood, I'd been relieved. We'd destroyed his cloning machines. Rachel had gone missing, and her absence had caught all of our attention. Chad had melted down, not publicly crying but losing all emotion altogether. He'd faded right in front of our eyes.

Those moments were when I'd finally understood how deeply my brother loved his woman. And I hadn't the slightest idea what to do for him.

Icahn was dead. I'd never looked further into it. I'd had to take care of Chad.

But then Rachel was returned to us, thanks to Deacon —a fact no one in my family was ever going to forget—and I should have thought about it then.

I hadn't.

Not once.

"What now?" What else was there really to ask?

My father got to his feet. "We call in the Warriors. We make a plan."

"Right." I nodded. "Dad, there's one thing more."

Outside, a dong sounded, our nightly call to dinner.

The mess halls would start to serve. Some of our people had families, and in their tent homes would sit down to eat together. Those without anyone would gather in the halls, acting like the community everyone wanted Genesis to be.

Even if it was sometimes the coldest, unfeeling group of humanity ever assembled in one spot.

"What is it?" He looked tired. How much longer could he do this? Chad had to take over soon, let Dad go back to fighting as a Warrior, teaching, or something else. "Micah? Get it out."

There it was. Those last words. I wasn't going to concern myself with what he did and didn't do. I'd get to it. *Fine.* "I wasn't alone down there. Brynna, the former Vampire, she was with me."

"Is that so?" He shook his head. "Not telling me would have been a huge detail to leave out."

"Well, that's why I didn't." This was what we were like all the time. Back and forth. Push and pull. Poking at each other. It was never going to be different.

"Fine." A muscle ticked in his jaw. "Great. Then she can help us."

"Ah." I backed away from the table, practically stumbling over a chair in back peddling away from my father. "I didn't get the impression helping us was part of her plans. She saved my life a couple of times. I think mostly because she doesn't like death. But... she doesn't come across as the kind of person who's simply going to take up a cause. I get the impression she has her own agenda."

My dad was quiet for a second. "We know she knows about the scientists. Margot does, too." My father's mention of the scientist we'd recruited reminded me just how far down this rabbit hole went. We'd recruited her after she'd saved Brynna. Everyone knew someone. "We'll, of course, speak with her. But that Vampire is on the ground, in the midst of this, and Margot has been with us for months."

My father had misjudged this situation to the point of completely misunderstanding it. I sighed. "When you're making your plans, I wouldn't count on Brynna as being a sure thing. She's more like…" What was the word from school? "A variable."

Patrick Lyons led men. He'd always done so by any means necessary. He used people's strengths and weaknesses to get what he wanted, even letting Rachel sacrifice herself to save us all. I shouldn't have been surprised by what he said next, except I was. When it came to my family, I really was as dumb as my parents thought.

"I plan for many different contingencies. If I decide to make a plan involving that Vampire, then she will help us."

I shook my head. "How exactly will you make her?"

"She will either want to help us, or there's something she wants we can use to persuade her, or…" his voice trailed off, and I wondered why he'd stopped. What did he think was going to happen that he hadn't wanted to say?

"Or?" I prompted him to continue. "Go on. Or. What?"

My father sighed. "Or you're going to use your pretty face for good for once, and you're going to seduce the girl into doing what you want. She's already saved your life a bunch of times. And really? Weren't you trained better than that? Fuck her into doing it then, if fucking her is what it takes. You're good at that, right?"

I went cold. My father planned to order me to fuck Brynna for the sake of Genesis. "What?"

My dad threw his hand in the air. "Maybe it won't come to you needing to take one for the cause. Maybe she'll be feeling altruistic."

"Patrick." From the back of the room Tiffani Endover,

fellow board member with my father and the wife of the late Keith Endover who had trained us all to be Warriors, spoke. "We had a meeting right?"

Of course she had heard. Of course she had.

I walked past her, heading out the door. "Tiffani."

She grabbed my arm. "Micah…"

I pulled out of her hand. I didn't want comfort right now or nice words. Because he couldn't be done with me, not yet. Of course, my father called out to me, "We've all had to do things that make us uncomfortable. If it comes down to it, I know you'll do the right thing."

I had to leave before I punched my own father in the face.

Five minutes later, my temper still roared so loudly I could hear my heartbeat in my ears. They were about to call a Warrior meeting that I would be expected to attend since I was here. Too many people had seen me. I couldn't hide, couldn't take off in enough time to avoid the thing altogether. I had to cool off. Find my fake face, the one I pulled out to make me look easy going and happy. I had to be that version of myself if I was going to sit in a room with the entire Warrior population of Genesis and not lose my damned mind.

I jumped up and down. I couldn't get drunk. There wasn't enough time. And there wasn't a girl around I could fuck fast enough to lose this edge. So that meant exercise. Good old fashioned work it out with sweat. I ran hard toward the woods. Top speed.

I was in great physical condition; probably the best of my life, and no mere jog was going to suffice this time. I tore forward like Werewolves chased me. I sprinted like the Vampires were gaining speed. I made my body so fast my high school gym teacher would have actually given me an A. I was fast. Always had been.

"Hey," someone shouted from behind, and I didn't stop. I needed to get so tired I couldn't think, couldn't...

"Micah." That voice again. It was Chad. I slowed down, my breath coming in and out in spurts. Okay, maybe I'd gotten close to how much I needed to run. I wasn't there yet but close, for sure.

I bent over at the knees. "Chad?"

My older brother caught up with me, also out of breath. How long had he been chasing me, and for that matter, how long had I been running? I turned around. I was way up on top of the hill east of Genesis. I'd really been moving. This was no easy trek.

"Fuck. Micah." My brother joined me in bending over at the knees. "What the hell?"

I lifted my head, forcing my breathing to slow. Chad so rarely cursed it was usually amusing when he did. I guessed I wasn't in the mood to laugh. "Need something?"

"You looked like death was chasing you, so I decided to help with whatever it was you were hauling ass to get away from."

Chad's words were enunciated by the panting he did in between each of them. Maybe the boy needed to up his cardio.

My big brother died in a Vampire lair deep beneath the earth two days walk from here. I hadn't made it that far yet in my exploration. He'd been made a bloodsucker. Brynna hadn't lied when she'd said Warriors could be turned. They'd managed to do so with my brother. He stood before me now because his wife had all but sacrificed her soul to Isaac Icahn to bring him back as a clone.

That time had been the definition of hell. There had never been an existence for me that didn't include Chad in some way. I should hate him. Living in his shadow hadn't been any fun. He was a straight A student, the perfect, responsible son, had gotten scholarships out the wazoo to go to college, fell in love with exactly the right girl and married her. He was the perfect Warrior and the heir to the unofficial Lyons throne.

The golden child from birth to death and then even in his second version of life.

He was moral. Upstanding. Funny. Kind. Smart. He knew his north, and he pointed himself toward it.

But I didn't hate him. Not even a little bit. I loved Chad. Fiercely. I'd follow him into hell and wouldn't even ask why.

"Dad wants me to fuck the Vampire girl, Brynna, to get her to do what we want." I paused. "If it comes to that. Guess he feels my own value in this situation is to drop my pants and fuck for the family."

Chad winced. He stood straight, and then he laughed. What the hell was funny? Finally, I asked him. "What are you finding laugh worthy?"

"Our father has hit a new low. Once upon a time, they were talking to us about abstinence. No sex before marriage. Respecting our future wives. Now it's go fuck a Vampire, Micah? Screw that. No one makes you sleep with anyone you don't want to. He can find another way, or I'll get Rachel and, together, we'll find another way. You're not some kind of prostitute he can send out on his behalf. You're his son."

I never questioned why I loved Chad so fiercely. But if I ever did, I'd just have to remember this moment. I didn't cry. I'd been pretty much trained since birth that only the death of a loved one warranted tears. I wanted to cry. My big brother still gave a damn.

"I... I think everyone might be overestimating how much sex I have."

Chad put out his hand in front of him. "Don't. I mean,

if you have to, then do. I guess. I've got no real interest, whatsoever, in knowing about your sex life."

I smirked. This was comfortable ground. "So is that why you waited? For Rachel? Because you wanted to respect your future wife."

"Yep." Chad was unapologetically unashamed of his life choices. He was proud of the idea he'd only know the love of one woman.

My path had gone quite differently, and my own history didn't bother me either. Love and I were not on the road to being best buds. I didn't think there was one girl out there for me. Not only one, anyway. Why would anyone want to settle for me? In small doses, I was all right to be around. On the long haul, I was bound to disappoint. I was not husband material.

"So what you're saying, fearless Warrior leader," I patted Chad on the back before continuing, "is I am allowed to say no to this assignment?"

He elbowed me in the side. "Yes. No one makes you sleep with anyone. Especially not some awful Vampire." He mock shuddered.

I opened and closed my mouth. Brynna wasn't awful. Not even a little bit. She was tiny and beautiful. She was brave, self-sacrificing, and sharp witted. I wasn't ready to tell Chad about her yet. She'd saved my life, many times it would seem. I didn't even know if I'd ever see her again. I hoped I would, but I wasn't going to analyze why.

It was possible we were about to miss our meeting because Chad and I sat on the top of the hill and watched the sun begin to dip on the horizon. I didn't know what Chad dwelled on, but as for me, I kept picturing the dark-haired former Vampire who brought with her long dead memories. What was she doing right now?

Chapter 3

As it turned out, we didn't miss the meeting. They'd had to wait for several Warriors to return from investigating the woods regarding the increased Vampire activity. Chad and I hadn't slacked off long enough. I sat in the chairs facing the panel of leaders in front of us. Currently, the council consisted of my father, Tiffani—who now knew my father intended to pimp me out—and Deacon, who had taken over a spot after Keith died.

He was our newest fearless leader, and from the way he squirmed in the chair, it was clear he wasn't yet comfortable with the attention. If the whispers around the room were any indication, not everyone was all that comfortable with him having assumed the role. That was okay. This wasn't a democracy. Not yet, anyway. In Genesis, the strongest ruled, and the title of strongest always fell to my father.

Patrick Lyons wanted Deacon, so Deacon was in. Truth be told, Deacon was perfect for the role. The kids loved him, and they were learning a lot.

My brother had attached himself to my side. I liked the alliance, for now. I was too old to need my big brother to protect me. That didn't mean I didn't want his company.

His wife, Rachel, sat on his other side. They linked hands, silent in their togetherness, but a constant unit nonetheless. Repeatedly, Rachel had proven she'd put Chad first. Even to her own detriment.

Of course, I had been her first crush. Long before she'd loved my brother, and even before, in this time, she'd dated the now deceased Werewolf, Jason, she'd had a thing for me. I'd thought she was cute, but she had been Tia's friend—which made her un-dateable—and then she'd seemed more like a sister than anything else.

The way things worked out was the best possible scenario. I was glad I'd never had the chance to fuck up our relationship. She was, officially, my sister now. It would be weird if we'd ever slept together.

Besides, the way she loved Chad... she'd never had those feelings for me.

Smart girl.

On my other side, Deacon's wife plopped down. She wasn't technically a Warrior. But our husbands and wives got to come to meetings if they wanted to. I was surrounded by friends—Glen, Peter, Johnny, my sister Tia, who almost never came to these things. Why hadn't I stopped to consider I had so many people here? Most of the time, I felt alone.

A little bit to our left was the civilian representative. My father had conceded that a non-Warrior could be present for our discussions to represent the needs of the non-Warrior when it was warranted. I guessed Isaac Icahn counted in that regard. He had destroyed all of our lives.

My father rose, and the room fell silent. Now, there was a display of power. All he had to do to quiet hundreds of people was stand. Anger and disgust warred with the silent hero worship I had always possessed for the man who fathered me. I was 22. At what point would I stop looking at him as a larger than life figure and see him only as the flawed human I knew he was?

Chad leaned closer then whispered. "Do you suppose he'll be ordering anyone else in this room to take one for the team?"

A grin spread over my face. Chad never used to be like this. Talking out of turn? It would have been unheard of. I might have been rubbing off on him. "Nope. That's just reserved for his flesh and blood."

"Sshh," Glen, my brother-in-law, hissed. "He'll never call out the two of you. Somehow this will be all my fault."

He wasn't wrong. Ever since Glen knocked up and married my sister when she was sixteen—which had to have been Tia's idea, not his—Glen took the hot end of my father's temper regularly. I was just the disappointing son. Glen had taken his baby girl and made her a mother before her 18th birthday.

That was, of course, perfectly legal under Genesis rules. The law recognized us as adults at 16. It made sense, considering most of us wouldn't see 30, much less 40.

"We eliminated Isaac Icahn and his cronies four years ago," my father finally spoke. Had it been *that* long? Endless days leading into endless nights, I'd somehow lost track of time. Four years. Wow. I didn't get to muse much longer. My father kept speaking. "We knew there was a possibility this day would come. The day he could be cloned again. We knew there was a possibility there were more cloning machines out there and, since we understand so little of how they work, it would be possible they'd have the capability to bring the man back."

Someone called from the back of the room. "Shit, Patrick. Has that happened?"

"They mean to bring him back. My son, Micah"—he indicated me with his hand as though anyone in the room might not know who I was—"overheard their plans in the Vampire lair this afternoon."

Gregory Smith, one of the older Warriors jumped to his feet. "Why didn't you kill them, Micah? Right then?"

I usually would make a flippant remark or ignore a question addressed to me like that. Who had time for bull-shit? But I was soul weary, and since I'd been asked a direct question, I'd give a direct answer.

"Killing humans isn't really part of my job description. Monsters, sure. I mean if I went and killed every human who bothered me, at least half this room would be dead."

My father didn't care for my answer. "Micah."

In front, Deacon snorted. "Half the room? Try three quarters. I'd be dead."

"Deacon." I guessed my father didn't like his remark either.

"Here's the thing. My killing those scientists was complicated by a few factors. The first being I wasn't going to do it. The second, I doubt very much if killing two would really accomplish anything. We have to find their central lair, and the only way we're going to do so is quietly and with a purpose."

Tiffani spoke, her voice calm amidst the wave of temper. "Why quietly?"

"It's a maze down there. Doors open and then vanish. It was set up to remain undiscovered. I can go down the same hallway three times and see different things each time. I asked Margot about it when she first gave me the preliminary map." The doctor who had once been forced to work with the scientists below ground was now on our own side. She wasn't here, which wasn't surprising. She was mostly kept at arm's length, given her less than stellar beginning. We weren't one hundred percent sure if we could trust her. And by we, I meant Dad. He wasn't sure.

I trusted her.

"And what did Margot say?" Tiffani still had the floor. I didn't know if it was because the whole room liked Tiffani so much or out of respect for Keith, but when his widow spoke, she was given the floor quietly.

Grateful for the opportunity, I finished my thought. "That's how it is down there. She didn't even really know all the ins and outs. She'd basically been dragged around. There is someone down there who will know. And it's recently been pointed out to me I might be equipped to cut her some kind of deal." I wasn't going to sleep with her, no matter what my father suggested. I'd get her to help some other way. "But if we all go traipsing down there ready to storm the proverbial castle, we're going to be seriously fucked." I shrugged and sat back down. "Up to you all, of course."

Chad groaned. "Killing half the room?"

Yeah, I was a real charmer.

⸻

I DESCENDED the ladder into the Vampire holding once again. The Warriors had decided I should take four to five others with me. Somehow, they deemed a small group as handling things quietly. They were out of their minds. I left ahead of their chosen few. I refused to play along as if they knew what they were talking about. Not down here.

Also, I had the strongest urge to see Brynna again. I

had questions in need of answering. She had to stop running. Plus, I couldn't remember the exact shade of brown her eyes were.

I nearly fell on top of Deacon, Chad, and Glen. I blinked, my mind catching up with the scene in front of me. What were they doing down here?

"What the ever-loving fuck?"

Deacon shrugged. "Well, we figured you'd never take your father's order and bring five people with you. Instead, you'd take off on your own."

Damn, I hated to be predictable.

"So we grabbed our shit and came along," Chad finished for him.

Glen grinned. "It was my idea."

"Well, he was the one who said it first." Deacon sighed. "I would have come on my own. I don't really think of the two of them as rule breakers."

"You sit on the council now, dipshit." Chad rolled his eyes. "If any one of us can't disobey orders, it's you."

I digested their words. They'd anticipated what I was going to do, which was weird enough, and left their homes —*wives*—to come help me. *Why?* "You know I can do this alone."

Chad patted me on the back. "Yes."

Was he humoring me?

A noise sounded, and suddenly, my father dropped down into the room. I practically swallowed my tongue. It was Chad who spoke. "Dad?"

"Well, I can see I wasn't wrong. I said my family is going to go do this on their own. And here you are."

I didn't know what he thought he was going to get out of this. We weren't teenagers he could order home. He could threaten to take away the rights and privileges we received from the safety of Genesis, I supposed, but doing so would really look bad for him.

"So you came to tell us to come home?" Chad shook his head. "Not happening."

"Nope." He patted my brother's back, and that was when his own backpack became visible.

Wait. Was he…? "Are you proposing to come?"

"Well, a large portion of my family is here. It only makes sense I'd join in. I'd have to be an idiot at this point to not know what you're doing. I'm going to help."

This was bullshit. My father hadn't done a mission like this in at least five years. There was something else going on.

"I'm not family," Deacon rolled his eyes.

"Oh, now, Deacon, you know we think of you as family."

I laughed. I couldn't help it. Until recently, he had detested Deacon. But, okay. Fine. Now maybe we were all family.

My father wasn't done. "At least as much as Glen here is."

Chad groaned, and a muscle ticked in Glen's jaw. I really didn't know how much longer my brother-in-law was going to put up with this crap.

"Get over it, Dad. You have a grandson from him. And another on the way. You should be kissing his ass for putting up with Tia at all."

My father totally ignored me. "Where is Rachel?"

"Not coming." Chad rocked back on his feet. "She's pregnant. I managed to talk her into staying home."

Silence fell over the group, and then seconds later, we exploded into noise. The whole time we were on the hill, he'd not said a word. Everyone patted him on the back, and my father hugged Chad like he'd single handedly saved the entire universe. I couldn't help my grin. Chad was going to be a daddy. The son of a bitch was going to have girls. I knew it.

I pulled him into a hug. "You should go home. You too, Dad. And Glen. And you Deacon. You all have families."

Glen shook his head. "You're our family. When are you going to get that? I can't go home to my wife and tell her I didn't do everything to help her brother. So let's get moving. Where do we get to meet this former Vampire?"

That was the thing. So far, she'd only found me. Not the other way around. "I don't know. She's made herself known to me twice. Apparently, saved my life three times I didn't know about. But if we head in the direction where I've encountered her, perhaps we'll have better luck."

We'd stepped into her zone. This was her world, and if she didn't want to deal with us, we'd never find her. The trick was going to be to make her think she did. I side-eyed my father. This was going to be hard as hell.

"I don't suppose you'd go home, Dad." It wasn't a question.

He raised his eyebrows. "Don't you want to spend time with the old man, Micah?"

"I can't imagine you want to spend time with me." I shook my head. "Never mind. Not the time or place." The last thing that was going to make Brynna come out was a bickering Lyons family.

If it were me out there in the dark, watching, I'd give us a wide berth and not get anywhere near this mess.

That was when it dawned on me. The fluorescent lights weren't flashing. Someone had changed them. I stared up at the solid light for a second, knowing everyone waited on me, watching.

"Micah?" Deacon wanted my attention. "You okay?"

"Who me?" I smirked at him. "I'm always okay."

Or at least I pretended to be.

━━

WE FINALLY LOCATED the room where I'd encountered the scientists bent on bringing back Icahn. It was still a mess, but something had changed. A panel on the floor was open. That was different. Someone had been in here since I left.

Squatting, I examined the opening. "This wasn't visible before."

"Icahn and his underground stuff." My father shook his head. "Just when you think you've gotten as low as you can, you find another layer."

Truth. "We don't know if this is Icahn. Any of the scientists could have made this mess."

"They're all scum." Glen scooted over, sticking his head in the hole. "They've got a ton of equipment in here. Score. I'm going down."

My brother-in-law leaped into the hole without giving it another look. I sighed. Glen got so excited by electronics. We had so little of it, and tech had been his passion in the Before Time. I hoped it wasn't all booby-trapped and I wouldn't need to yank him out of there. Or, worse, he died and then I'd have to explain to my loose cannon sister why I didn't watch Glen better.

We really did all obsess about having to deal with Tia.

Chad and I made eye contact then he called down. "Are you okay?"

"Yep."

My father shook his head. "Amazing you have all survived this long. You're supposed to be the elite Warriors. You simply jump into holes?"

"Pretty much." Chad shrugged. "Holes. Battles. Death traps. We jump. A lot."

I rolled my eyes. Chad never jumped into anything without thinking about it first. He was pissed at my father, and this was how he was dealing with it. I didn't like to be the cause of friction in the family, at least not for other people.

I patted Chad on the back. "You do, Big Brother, but you're super Warrior. I'm probably hanging back, not doing much."

He furrowed his brow. "Hardly. You..."

I didn't let him finish. I followed Glen. Deacon, who had been pretty quiet, swore. "Damn it, Micah."

I looked around. Glen was bent over some old computers. "These are floppy disks. Remember these?"

I shook my head. "Not really."

"Yeah, they were old even back then. How long was all of this being plotted?"

Too long. "And how did we end up in the middle of it? We were a bunch of kids from New Jersey."

Glen raised his head to smirk at me. "I was from Rockland County in New York. I'd only lived near you guys in Jersey for a year and a half."

That was right. He'd met Tia that year in high school. She'd pretty much chased him tirelessly while Chad and I ran point, trying to stop her from going too far. "How did they get you? I mean, they came for us in the middle of the night. Dragged us out of bed. Dad even fired his gun."

"I... I was there with Tia."

I gaped at him. "You were in her bedroom? Never mind. Don't tell me." They were married. They had a baby. This shouldn't make me feel like I wanted to beat him to death.

"They found me there and then went and got my parents. It's all so… surreal to even think about."

These were not memories I liked to visit. I strode over to the shelves. There were books and photo albums. I pulled one out and flipped through it. They were pictures of Vampires. In all states of development. Vamps looked downright human when they were first changed, and then their features got more and more distorted, more monster-like.

Had Brynna done the same?

Did she look more Vampire or human now?

How did it work?

There was an oomph as Chad jumped down to join us. He looked around. "Oh cool. Are those floppy disks? How retro."

Of course he remembered them. I rolled my eyes. One of the Vampires in the picture clawed at her own face. What was wrong with her? These poor photographed people. I swallowed. That was right. They were people. Like Brynna was a person.

And yet, we had to kill them because they would kill us.

How did any of this make any sense?

Deacon jumped down, followed by my father. I looked up at the ceiling. "You realize not one of us considered how we were getting up from here. I mean. It's not like there's a ladder."

My dad sighed. "That's what comes from just jumping."

"You leaped without looking, too." Deacon patted him on the back.

Personally, I was done with the 'leaping before we looked' conversation and the underlying things we weren't saying. The possible metaphor of the whole dang thing was an oversimplification anyway.

"Someone got down here and left again. That's why it was opened. They got out some other way." Or they were still down here. I wasn't lost in my memories, so I doubted it was Brynna. I turned around, searching the possibilities. "Glen, leave that here. We can come back for it another time."

He grimaced but set aside the box of parts. Regret filled my stomach. He really loved to get ahold of items he could use to create basic technology these days.

"Seriously, we'll come back." I hated disappointing people, and damn, why were they listening to me anyway? I was never in charge. When had this happened? Even my father looked at me for direction. "Everyone touch the walls. Look for hidden levers or moveable panels—some way whoever came down here could exit."

I hoped I was right. If that didn't happen, I was going to look even dumber than I usually did. Everyone started touching the walls, and ultimately, it was me who found the secret door. The wall gave with a click, illuminating another hallway. I sighed. All this time, there had been a whole other level beneath me, and I'd no idea.

Glen smiled broadly. "How cool."

He hadn't been doing this for weeks. "So much for my map."

"The reality is you were never going to make a map." My dad pushed past me toward the hall. "You'd have gotten bored with it."

Chad followed him out. "He hadn't yet."

I grabbed Chad's arm. "Taking my side has always been pointless."

"That doesn't mean I'm going to stop doing it when you're right. He's not the only stubborn member of the family. You've never been stubborn, which is why you can't win with him. I get him completely."

What the hell? I wasn't stubborn? I ended up walking behind Glen and next to Deacon down the new hallway. I was pretty darned stubborn. Wasn't I?

"Not there," a voice called out into the darkness, stopping us all in our tracks. I knew the low yet feminine sound well by now. It was Brynna. She stepped out in front of my dad, all elegant movement. Memory shoved at me.

I was ten years old and playing baseball. I'd been a big star that season. I could hit, and when I did, the ball left the field. I was Homerun Micah. Except when my father was there. Every time I swung, I missed. I could never turn around to see him. I knew the look on his face...

Utter disappointment.

I swung. I missed. Tears pressed in my eyes, and I shoved them back. Lyons didn't cry.

Almost everyone around me groaned, Chad doubling over to hold his knees. Yes, it hurt the first time. It really did. Deacon seemed to be okay, too. He shook his head. "Such an odd sensation. I forgot all about tripping down those stairs."

"I'm sorry." She looked away. "If I could make it otherwise, I would."

I pushed past the others to get closer to her. "Why does it happen?"

"You'd have to ask Margot. I simply live with the knowledge that it does." She pointed behind her. "In a minute, you'll all get your Warrior Vampire signal. A room full. Hungry and needing their drugs. Makes them more violent. You don't want to go there."

My father was at my side. "You must be Brynna."

"I must be." She didn't smile at him, and her always hard to read face showed annoyance for a second. "You must be Patrick Lyons. Leader of Genesis. Father of five."

His mouth fell open. "You know me?"

"I know lots of things." Her gaze moved past me to Chad behind me. "Good to see you again, Chad. Deacon. Glen, this is a first time."

Chad rocked back on his heels. "When did we see each other before?"

"When you were a Vampire. Before you died. And yet you are here. Cloned. Welcome back?"

He shook his head. "I don't have any memories of what you're talking about. I don't remember dying. I don't remember being cloned. I feel as though... I've always been."

She didn't have a response, so maybe there wasn't one to make.

Deacon looked between them. "And she knew me, too, when I was Vampire bait."

A sudden memory hit me, but this time it wasn't my own. A little boy, light brown hair, ran down a hallway screaming at the top of his lungs. Vampires watched. He skidded past them, searching for his parents and what was left in his wake was overwhelming sadness.

The emotion almost brought me to my knees. I gasped and everyone looked at me. The little boy was... Deacon.

I jolted, looking around. Had no one else seen the horror but me? I'd experienced Deacon's terror alone. My pulse was in my ears, and my gaze fell on Brynna. Her eyes were huge.

"Did you see that, Micah?" Her voice was barely a whisper. "How is that happening? Why is that happening? You shouldn't be in my head."

My father had clearly had enough. "Brynna, we need to speak to you."

She sucked in a breath, her expression steeling, unreadable. "I can't imagine what we'd say to one another."

I knew in my gut she was about to run. "Don't go." I

clasped her arm. Her skin was soft, like silk, and for a second, we both stared at where I held her. I hoped I wasn't bruising her. I swallowed. "Please."

She was quiet. "Okay, Micah. I won't."

That was good. The question remained, however, about what the hell I would say next.

Chapter 4

"Brynna," I said her name again, even as I held onto her arm. "We need your help with our Isaac Icahn problem."

She sucked in her breath. "They're re-cloning him."

"Yes. We only destroyed the cloning machines we knew about. They obviously have more."

Brynna sighed. "They have hundreds of them, at least. And those are just the ones I've seen. You aren't destroying all of them. I'm going to suggest you don't even try."

"Young lady," my father tried to cut in.

I spoke before he could finish. Nothing that Dad began with *young lady* ended well. "Will you help us?"

I waited for the *what's in it for me*. I knew she would have to ask. It was how the world worked. *What's in it for me?* She visibly swallowed, then said, "Okay. But I have one request."

Here it came. What did she want? She had us by the balls. We'd give it to her. My father wouldn't even object. "What's that?"

"Don't ever call me a monster again. Please."

My heart fell to my stomach. Guilt pressed on my

shoulders and threatened to take me to the ground. I'd really hurt her. "I would never have done it again anyway."

Was it possible to have a *moment* in front of others?

It was like she was the only other in the universe and we were alone in a dark quiet room, not down the hall from Vampires with my best friend and family watching us.

She sucked in a breath. "Even when you think it."

"I won't think it." I meant it. I said it, and I meant it. *Damn it.*

"You will." Her voice shook. "Even when you do. Please don't say it."

I cupped her face in my palms and locked gazes with her. "I won't."

She nodded. "Thank you, Micah. Yes, I'll help you."

"Thank you, Brynna."

The world pounded back at us. I was suddenly keenly aware of everyone else in the room breathing. I dropped my hands from her face then stepped back. My breathing was shallow, and my heart beat too fast. Fuck. What was the matter with me?

She spoke again, which was good because I wasn't sure I could. "We will have to go past the Vampires to get to where you need to be."

My father answered her. "We'll kill them. That's what we do."

I had to ask. "Is that going to be a problem?" She'd been a Vampire. She had... unusual abilities. Was she going to try and stop us?

Brynna withdrew a step. "Honestly? For them it will be a relief." Her voice broke. "An escape from all of the memory. All of the pain. All of the blood. Please try to be quick and kind. I'll wait for you. On the other side of the room. You won't see me till it's over."

I tried to let my mind catch up to what she said, but no

one else seemed as bothered by her words. Hadn't they heard her breath hitch? Her voice break? Didn't they care?

With my father leading, we headed toward the fight, but I only had eyes for Brynna. One second she was there, the next a blur of movement as she vanished. I sighed. How was I supposed to keep track of her when she moved so swiftly?

Chad grabbed my arm. "I thought you weren't going to do what Dad told you to do."

I didn't follow him. "I'm not."

"Then what was that?"

Deacon patted him on the back. "Chad filled me in on what your dad wanted. So, I'm in the loop here." They'd *discussed* it? "Boy here just fell hard. Like over a cliff. He doesn't even know it yet."

A range of emotions passed over Chad's expression, ending with him scrunching up his face. "Fuck. You fell for the…"

I put my hand over his mouth. I didn't know what kind of hearing Brynna had. And, in any case, I wasn't at all sure that what he was about to say was true. "Not now. Later."

Way later. When I could… think.

Chad nodded, and I dropped my hand. Whatever my brother was going to say, he'd keep to himself now. At least until a more appropriate time. In the meantime, I needed my heartrate to calm down a little bit. I was going to fight angry Vampires. I couldn't do it this… tense.

There was no time for me to pull my shit together. Totally oblivious to all of this, Glen pulled open the door, unleashing the raving masses onto us. My Vampire alert hit me hard. Sometimes I had to fight whether I was ready or not.

And this was a lot more understandable than the woman I'd promised to never refer to as a monster again.

⊏⊐

I STAKED my last Vampire and jumped left, prepared to take on more. But they were all gone. Glen threw up in the corner. He puked after battle. Always did. Every time. We'd all gotten used to it by now. At least he was in the corner. One time, he'd puked on my shoes.

Chad bounced from foot to foot. He wasn't winded and neither was I. Deacon leaned against the wall. My father spun in a circle, his eyes were wide. He'd performed, but it had been a while since he'd had to engage in straight combat.

"It's over." When my father didn't respond, I tried again. "Dad, it's over."

"Oh." My dad quit looking for Vampires and ceased moving. He took an audible breath. "Yes. Of course."

I went to him, calmness making me familiarly numb. This was what happened after battle. The blissful nothingness. I strolled past, patting my father on the shoulder. I almost hoped he criticized me. Right now, it wouldn't matter at all.

"Good work, boys."

Chad responded. "Thanks, Dad."

I wasn't interested in his gratitude. Just whatever came next. The room was empty save for the dust of the undead. If I'd had time to think it through, I would have stolen some clothing off them before we got down to it. But I hadn't been in that frame of mind.

Brynna appeared before me, quickly wiping tears from her eyes. The blissful numb faded immediately. "What's wrong?"

She shook her head. "Nothing."

"Obviously something is wrong. You're crying."

Brynna visibly swallowed. "You really are as kind as he said you were."

"As who said I was?"

She groaned. "Listen…"

A loud rumbled started above our heads. I looked up in time to see plaster raining down. What in the ever-loving *fuck*? Brynna gasped. "Cave in."

That was the last thing I heard. The world went black with a boom. Or maybe it was the other way around. Maybe it went boom first. I didn't know. Just… nothing.

———

I WOKE to my name being repeated. Over and over. I forced my eyes open even though I really wanted to slip back into nothingness. But someone was calling me, so I had to wake. My ears rang, my throat was dry, and the world didn't seem right. It tilted somehow.

Brynna kneeled next to me. We were… *where were we?* "What happened?"

It hurt to talk. Why did it feel like I'd swallowed concrete?

"The ceiling came down." She pointed to her left. "Collapsed. I grabbed you. And I got us a little bit away. Unfortunately, we are trapped on all sides. The ceiling is partially down. It's like we're in a box."

Well, that was incredibly bad news. Though dizzy, I managed to get to my knees. She and I were okay for now. I was pretty sure I was going to puke, but my need to vomit could wait a second. "The others?"

"I don't know." She looked down. "I only grabbed you. I'm sorry. I was next to you and…"

My throat tightened, but I wouldn't let in thoughts of their deaths right now. I had no way to confirm they were gone, and most likely, they'd jumped away. We were good at that. I touched her arm. "This is four."

She shook her head. "I don't follow."

I held up four fingers. "That's how many times I'd be dead if not for you. Oh no, the last time with the scientists. Five." I changed the number of fingers I held up.

She sat back on her rear. "I might not have been successful this time. We might yet die."

If she wanted to be a downer, didn't mean I had to follow her lead. "Well, I've lived well past my expiration date. I should be what? Two hundred? Three hundred years old now?"

I crawled over to the wall and leaned against it. Silence followed me. Then she finally said, "There's something I should tell you."

Something else? "What's that, beautiful?"

She furrowed her brow. "Um, at some point, I'm going to have to feed."

I pointed to my backpack. I still wore it. "We can share rations. When I'm clearer in the head, we'll start brainstorming a way out. If we're careful, we have days of food and water."

Brynna looked down. "No, I mean, I'm going to need blood."

I was slower than I should have been because it took me a second to follow what she said. "You're not a Vampire anymore." Had she hit her head?

She sighed. "They didn't entirely cure me. There will be part of me that is always Vampire. I am going to have to consume blood. It doesn't have to be human and even if it is, I don't have to kill anyone. I eat and drink regular substances, too. But this is a factor. About once a week. I'm due soon."

I had to fight to concentrate. I was most certainly concussed. But that didn't matter right now. Brynna had to feed. "How soon?"

"Today." She looked away. "I'm sorry." She buried her face in her knees. It was harder to understand her, but she continued speaking. "The doctors initially said the need would stop. It hasn't, but every month I hope. I'm sorry, Micah. This is all my fault."

It would be easy to let her take the blame for this. I knew better than most how it was to be responsible for the world's ills. Okay, maybe she could have not let her blood-lust go so long, but it wasn't like she knew she was going to be in this mess.

"You didn't make the ceiling come down. You didn't get us caught in here. Nothing about this is your fault. In fact, you didn't make yourself a mons—*Vampire*. Let's go ahead and blame Isaac Icahn and everyone like him."

She lifted her head. "I have a hard time reconciling you. In Chad's memory, he saw you as so smart, kind, funny. He envied you your ease with people. Thought the world of you. He still does, obviously. I can see it. Just now, you were all those things. And yet earlier, you showed you can also be cruel. Who are you Micah Lyons?"

That was the question of the day. Who was I? "Right now I'm a guy with a throbbing headache."

"Fair enough." She put her head against her knees again.

I didn't have to be an asshole, even with my headache. "Who am I? I'm a guy who was born in New Jersey. Down by the shore. A long time ago. I don't even know if there is a beach anymore. I had my heads in the clouds. I was a lousy student. I was frozen when I was seventeen. Woke up still seventeen. Now I'm twenty-two. I don't even know who I'd have been if none of this crap happened. If Chad has those nice thoughts about me, it's because Chad is such a nice guy. He sees the best of everyone. I don't." I sighed. Wasn't that the truth? "Who are you?"

Brynna raised her gaze. "Well, I was a Vampire. I…"

I raised my hand to stop her. "Before then. Who were you?"

I didn't think I could stomach thoughts of her Vampire life right then. Waves of nausea rippled over me every time I moved. I was really going to vomit soon whether I liked it or not. We didn't have to hurry along the process.

"I was a twenty-year-old woman attending Columbia as an undergraduate in New York City."

I laughed. "So you're a smartie. Go on."

"I was." She didn't even sound the least bit modest about it. Owning her intelligence was seriously hot. Oh hell, what was wrong with me? I'd blame the concussion, but it'd started before the walls fell in. "I was studying comparative literature and society."

I choked. "You weren't planning on eating after you got out college?"

Her grin could have lit up the whole underground maze. "I was planning on teaching. I was going to get a Masters and a Ph.D."

I couldn't remember the last time I talked like this. "You *liked* school that much?"

From the little bit of fluorescent light creeping in through cracks in the downed ceiling, it became obvious that Brynna's gaze grew distant. "I loved it. I understood it. There was never a time I couldn't make sense of school. I loved writing papers. What authors said, what they meant, how they could be interpreted—it all seemed so important. Like the *Allegory of the Cave*. Plato."

I shook my head. "I'm not smart. I don't know what that is."

I liked how discussing the subject animated her. "You were what? Seventeen when you were frozen? I don't know if they do Plato in every high school. I attended a really challenging academy in New York City. We did college level work as juniors and seniors."

She wasn't smart… she was *smart*.

"A New York City girl." They were like unattainable magical creatures to Jersey boys. So perfectly put together, so sophisticated.

"I never even went to New Jersey before I was changed. Not even to go to the mall."

I clasped at my heart. "Oh, the way you say mall with such derision. The malls in Jersey were epic. Things of beauty. You could have gotten a pretzel anytime you wanted."

Her face fell. "Anyway, yeah. That's who I was. I'm too old for you."

I wasn't going to dissuade her about my attraction. She'd have to be stupid to not realize my interest, considering I continued flirting with her while my head pounded so loudly it could have been a mariachi band playing a tune.

"Let's do the math. I was frozen at seventeen. Woke up seventeen. I've aged. I'm twenty-two. You were turned at twenty. You were fixed a year ago when you conceivably started aging. So you're twenty-one. And even if you were older, that's hot."

She laughed so hard she threw her head back. "I really like you, Micah. I think you're more how Chad sees you than you see you."

A dripping noise in the distance punctuated the silence. Somewhere, water made its way along the stone. Drip.

Drip. It traveled through small spaces, never stopping, always finding the next space to fill until it was finally absorbed. As destructive as it was life saving.

I shouldn't be left alone with my own thoughts. "Tell me more about Plato. I interrupted you. I might not be able to understand. I was bad at school."

"School isn't for everyone. That doesn't mean you weren't smart. In Chad's memories, you were a pilot. You had learned to fly the second it was legal. You wanted to be in the military. Like your father."

I rubbed my eyes. "Dad was an Army Ranger. I wanted to fly Navy planes. But yes, sort of. Plato. In the dumbest terms possible."

She scooted over next to me. "Someone did a number on you, didn't they?" Brynna's dark hair fell down the front of her body. I wanted to run my fingers through it, but I didn't. She'd been a Columbia undergraduate with a bright future ahead of her. All of my flirting aside, she'd be bored with a dolt like me soon enough. Losing her would hurt. I tried really hard to avoid emotional pain. Why look for it when there was so much freely given?

"Plato. He uses Socrates as a character and Socrates goes on to describe these people. They've been chained up their whole lives. They're forced to look at the same wall, a blank one. They have a fire behind them and when objects are moved in front of the fire it casts shadows on the wall. They name them. The shadows are what those people know of life. Plato goes on to say in order to be educated, to be a philosopher as he would call it, is to escape your cave and see those shadows for what they are—falsehoods. Those people have no idea they should want to leave the cave, but when they do, they discover the fire. Yet, even in freedom, we are forever stuck knowing things through the lens by which we see them."

Was such a thing possible? Could any of us actually ever really know the truth, or was our existence already shaped and therefore determined by where we sat in life? Deacon's wife hadn't known anything except for her small town of Geronimo until we arrived at her doorstep. We had accepted the truths Icahn gave us because we had no reason to doubt. And we'd never had any idea Vampires lived in memory and were sad.

Could I accept the new reality as it was, or was I going to be stuck in my cave?

"What are you thinking about?"

I blinked. I guessed I'd gone quiet for too long. Embarrassment never sat well with me. I smirked. "Nothing. What you were talking about, it's all way above my head."

She chewed on her lower lip. "Somehow, I don't think so."

"Then you'd be wrong."

I expected her to snap at me. People usually did when I dismissed them or their opinions. Instead, she leaned her head on my shoulder. "Is this okay? I don't have to touch you if you'd prefer."

I liked it. "I'm going to close my eyes."

"I don't think you should. Isn't that one of the concussion rules?"

She might have been right, but that wasn't what my exhausted, nauseated self wanted to hear. "You know your almost degree in comparative literature that didn't send you to medical school?"

"Grouchy when you're hurt. Got it. Close your eyes. Fine by me. If you never wake up, at least they can't say I killed you."

I forced my eyes to stay open. "Fine. Passive-aggressive much?"

"I can guilt with the best of them." She was silent for a

second. "Thank you. I haven't talked to anyone like this since I came back to myself. It was all medical, and abuse, and trying not to die. Then escaping. I've been alone. And... touching someone—hanging out with them. Thank you."

I didn't like her gratitude. I'd never been comfortable with simple thank yous, and Brynna doing it made me even less sure of myself. "Stop saying thank you. I haven't done anything."

"Okay, if you say so." She gasped, covering her mouth and darting away from me.

I sat up. "What's wrong?"

Tears streamed down her face. "It's the need for blood. I have it now. I need it. I don't know what to do. I'm .."

I held out my wrist. "If it won't kill me, then take what you need."

The second my words registered in her dark eyes, she swallowed hard. "You're sure?"

"Well, it wouldn't be my first choice of what to do, but yeah, let's do it. You have to eat. I'm the only available source of it here. Have at it. My blood is your blood."

As she'd done before, she moved so fast I could barely watch her. Brynna took my wrist in her hand. Fangs descended in her mouth. I was transfixed. It should be gross and horrifying, only it wasn't. This was different than most Vampires. Her face was human. She was beautiful. There was a glow to her eyes that hadn't been there before.

She brought my wrist to her mouth. Could she feel how fast my heart beat? My pulse raced in anticipation.

Brynna bit down, breaking the skin fast. I sucked in my breath. The slight pinch lasted only seconds, but no pain followed. She drank, and I closed my eyes. My cock hardened fast. Well, that was unexpected. Pleasure pushed through me. I moaned like I was deep inside of her. This felt personal, maybe more so than any sex I'd ever had.

She touched the side of my face, and I opened my lids to meet her gaze. There was heat in it. Was she turned on, too? Did this happen every time? Fuck, I didn't want to know. I just wanted this. I wanted her.

I extended my neck, pointing to it with my free hand. "There instead. Please."

It would be... closer.

She released my wrist, then slid closer until she pressed against me. Once. She licked my neck *once*. My hips lifted off the ground against her groin. Brynna moaned before she bit my neck, sucking on my blood. Yes, that was what I wanted. My head didn't hurt. There was only pleasure. There was only Brynna.

I. Was. So. Fucking. Hard. How was I going to live through this? My cock throbbed in my pants. She pulled back, panting. "If I take any more, I'm going to hurt you."

I rolled her under me, practically tearing at her shirt. "If you don't want me, say so. I'm out of my mind with need for you, desire. Is it a blood thing?"

She nodded. "Yes, to wanting you. No, to a blood thing. Never this way before. Trust me."

I did, which was so weird because I didn't even know her at all yet. Fuck, I couldn't think when I was this hard. Instead, we undressed each other, slowing down from the frantic need to touch and kiss. Brynna smiled at me, and suddenly I became twice the man I actually was. Did she like how I looked naked? Was I... good looking to her?

Her breasts were round and perfect. I held them in my hands, feeling the utter luckiness every bastard who ever got to do this with a woman should feel. Somewhere along the way, I'd forgotten how lucky I was I got to do this. And as it was, I couldn't remember ever having done it before.

I kissed down her body until I was at her pussy, and she writhed beneath me. "I love foreplay, Micah, but now I just want you. Please. Fuck me like I mean something to you."

You do. I needed to tell her, but words had gone away. Instead, I grabbed a condom from the bag next to me, somehow got it on with shaking hands, and pushed inside of her waiting warmth. I cried out, the sound mixing with hers. I kissed her, I had to.

In and out I moved until we both panted, and I could hardly breathe. She squeezed me between her legs, and I was done. Thankfully she was, too, because I couldn't hold back. This was pleasure. This was… everything.

The world exploded between us. Or maybe it only felt like it.

Chapter 5

Lying on the ground shouldn't have been comfortable, but I was too sated to care. Brynna rested against my side, her eyes closed. My neck throbbed, which was better than my head, and now that I thought about it, so did my wrist. I lifted my arm to look at the wound. It had closed up. No one would know she had bitten me, one time because I'd practically demanded it.

Brynna was out cold.

What in the hell had all of the madness been about?

I stared down at her. She was lovely, pale skin and dark lashes displayed so clearly through... How come the light shining through the cracks was so bright? So visible? And why hadn't I thought of it before?

Well, because I was concussed and horny.

I eased her away from me, but she didn't stir. Maybe giving into the bloodlust exhausted her. Or maybe I'd fucked her into oblivion. Oh, screw that, she'd fucked me into oblivion. I threw on my boxers and walked in the direction of the light. We weren't in the pitch black. There was a fluorescent glow to the room like the stupid ones in all the hallways. Where was it coming from? Couldn't just be the cracks.

I walked forward, my eyes on the ceiling. How had having sex with Brynna cured my concussion? I thought I might solve the light question more easily. I stopped as soon as the reason occurred to me. Several of the rocks above our heads were loose. That was bad in the sense that they might come down on us, but it was equally good news, since I could probably get us out of here doing the same thing.

I stepped back. The question was: if I moved the few loose stones, was the whole damn thing going to come down on my head? I wasn't an engineer, but I had listened pretty intently to the things the engineering corps said at Genesis. A part of me wished I worked with them regularly rather than being a Warrior, but my life choices hadn't been my own.

Apparently, when I'd tried to kick the ass of the guys kidnapping me all those years ago, it had served as an audition to be part of Icahn's Warrior protection squad. Yay me. We'd evolved without Icahn, and hopefully, we would all get to be more someday.

Or at least Chad and Tia's kids could.

I scratched my head. Making all of that a possibility would be better served if I got dressed, and I wasn't going to bring the ceiling down on Brynna's head while she slept. After pulling on my hastily shed clothes, I knelt to wake her. First time for everything, I supposed. Most often I wanted women to sleep through my leaving. Everything about this former Vampire was different, and I didn't know why.

She had the softest skin. I kissed her lightly, once, then twice, on the cheek. She sighed, her eyes fluttering open. "Um. Hi. I guess I passed out."

"I did, too, for a little while. But I might be about to kill us, and I thought you might want to be up for it."

"Oh." She rubbed her eyes. "Um. Okay."

Her cheeks turned red, and the feeling of being a tool rushed through me. I'd had incredible sex with this woman, and now I was acting like nothing had happened at all. I grabbed her shirt and handed it to her. I would miss the sight of her naked body, but it was better to converse fully dressed whenever possible.

"That was pretty incredible." I sat and let her get dressed, averting my eyes so she could have some privacy. "Ah, does the heat always happen when you feed? Every time?"

I might kill someone if it did. Who were these other people she was fucking into unconsciousness? I… *Fuck, I'm becoming a caveman.* I was in basically what amounted to a cave, and suddenly, I wanted authority over who Brynna did and didn't sleep with? I had to get my shit together and fast.

She cleared her throat. "No, never before. Mostly it's been about finding someone to feed off, basically knocking them out to do it, and making sure they were okay before I left. Nothing has been easy or remotely hot before now. Let's face it, I wanted you before I fed off you. Maybe it was more about that. I think you wanted me, too."

I wasn't going to lie. "Pretty badly."

She rose. "Well, now that we've gotten our need for each other out of our system, what's going on with the ceiling?"

Not yet. Now that I had opened the door to post-coital discussion, we were going to talk. "How did you fix my head?"

She raised her eyebrows slowly. "I didn't. I'm not the

magical healing Vampire girl. Whatever happened with your head had nothing to do with me."

I could see her then, in my head, the way memories came to me now because of her. She stood on a hillside. I couldn't see her, only those around her, Vampires traveling downward toward a village full of people. Or at least it *was* full of people. She wanted to weep. Everyone there would be dead soon. Or made like them.

Brynna didn't know what she'd done to deserve this existence.

I grabbed her arm. "This isn't your fault."

She looked away. "How are you seeing my memories?"

"Just lucky that way, I guess." I rose. Okay, post-sex chatting was over. She was annoyed I could see what she remembered, yet I still missed some key pieces of information, like what and how she did the things she could. We weren't going to do be biting or fucking again, although thinking about it made me harden, and now we really should talk about the ceiling.

I pointed up. "The light. See how it's getting through the two rocks? I'm thinking if I pull them down, we can maybe get out. Or at least you can because of your Vampire super speed and what not?"

She eyed the spot. "I can move fast. I'm not stronger than you, and I can't particularly jump. This isn't going to be a superhero thing where I run up the walls. That being said, if you can really get those stones down, I can probably get up there if you hoist me. And then I'll find something for you to climb up."

I thought her idea sounded like our best option. I went to my backpack. There were certain things I never took out of it, and rope was one of them. "I've never been a cowboy. I have no experience hoisting or lassoing anything. This might take a minute."

She scrunched up her nose. "I think you'd be served best by trying to simply get it up and over. Then we kind of tug on both sides?"

Her suggestion sounded as good as anything else I might try. I threw the rope up, and it fell down on my head. I kept my face blank even as I winced inside. There was nothing like letting the best sex of your life see how much of an incompetent jackass you really were.

I set about to try again.

IT TOOK four hours to get the rope where I needed it. I held on to one side, and Brynna took the other. By the time I'd done it, I was dizzy. We needed to bring down the rock, but I needed a second.

Brynna ran to my pack and pulled out one of the packages of dried meat I'd brought along. It didn't taste good. The days of jerky were long over. God, I missed grocery stores. Yet, it would do.

She handed it to me. "You lost blood. And you might still be concussed."

I took a bite from the package. "You need to eat, too." I handed her half, and she took it. We stood there, chewing the hard dried meat, and she was right, my dizziness subsided.

"Thanks." She swallowed her last piece.

"Really gross, right?" The only thing that would improve it would be some beer. I was fresh out of alcohol. Or maybe everything tasted fine with beer because the beer was so all consuming. I shook my head. No need to dwell.

She winked at me. "Favorite food from back then?"

Good question. "Pizza. Of course."

Brynna rolled her eyes. "Oh, of course. I forgot. I was talking to a guy. You would say pizza. With all the food in the world you remember pizza."

She took one end of the rope. I took the other. "When we pull, jump back as fast as you can." I wanted to remind her before we went any further with this insanity. "There is nothing wrong with pizza. New York pizza was almost as good as Jersey pizza."

Brynna put a hand on her hip. "I am faster than you. The Vampire thing. And Jersey pizza couldn't touch New York pizza."

We tugged together, and I could feel the rock move ever so slightly. Okay, this wasn't going to be a one-two-three thing. It was going to take some time. "So what does a sophisticated New Yorker think about eating from the old days?"

"That's the thing. One small benefit of being a Vampire was I didn't have to only think about it. I could remember the food. If I wanted to, I could travel back to Gotham Grill and eat risotto again. I could taste the truffles. I could... I could visit other people's food memories. Like... your mother's pot roast."

For a second, I stopped breathing, and then I couldn't hold back my laughter. Bland. Chewy. I used to flush it down the toilet, which I once clogged in the attempt and then got punished for doing. "Oh gross. I don't miss that."

Her face fell. "Chad loved it."

"Yeah, Chad's a kiss ass even in his memory." I loved my brother to death, but I wouldn't want his taste buds if he liked that pot roast. "Come on, let's pull."

We did. Over and over, until it was clear the rock was coming down. One more yank, and it happened. I darted backward, and fortunately, my idea worked. It also didn't bring the rest of the ceiling with it, although with the amount of dust it kicked up, it might as well have.

"You okay?" Brynna stood right in front of me, swatting away the dust-filled air with her hand.

"That moving fast thing you do is weird and kind of cool at the same time. Yes, I'm fine." I looked up. "Big enough hole to get through now."

She ran a hand through her hair. "Right. Okay. Hoist me up."

I put my hands together, she stepped on them, and up she went. Brynna pulled herself up. "That's some impressive upper body strength."

"Right, well I've been a Vampire for hundreds of years. We lost a lot of things, but not muscle mass."

She pushed her head to the edge of the hole. "I'll be back to get you out. Hold steady."

It wasn't like I had anywhere to go. "Yeah, I'll do my best with that. Hey, Brynna, risotto? You were rich, too? Smart, beautiful, New Yorker, and rich?"

Her grin was slow. "I was the complete picture, wasn't I? None of that matters anymore. I'm some freak of nature that came back from being a Vampire to find nothing in the world for her at all. Don't get into trouble while I'm gone."

I waited until she was gone to really obsess over what she'd said. It shouldn't not matter who we were before. I refused to believe the first seventeen years of my life were a waste. All those people I knew back then weren't nothing simply because all of this had happened.

A surge of anger I couldn't control and didn't see coming moved through me, and I punched the wall. I yelled out as pain shot up my arm. Yeah, that was a jackass thing to do. I'd broken my hand. Oh what the fuck was wrong with me?

I walked around, shaking it every time it hurt, which was a lot, until I'd paced the room several times. I stared up the hole. Brynna wasn't back. Fuck me. Had she left me down here? I bent over to breathe through my pain. I could take a whole lot. I'd been shot once. Stabbed. All in the name of Genesis. Why did my hand hurt so much?

It would be just my luck. Meet the Vampire girl. Have sex with her. Abandoned by the same hot Vampire in a cavern. Thus ended the great Micah Lyons. I…

"Hey." She poked her head down. "Move back. I found a ladder. They have everything down here. I think they thought they might have to live here some time. Anyway, ladder. I'll lower it. Took me half a second. Why do you look like that?"

I forced myself to calm. "Like what?"

She scowled at me. "Micah."

"Fine, I broke my hand." She didn't need to hear the rest of it. "Lower the ladder."

I backed away, and she lowered it. Although every move I made with my hand hurt, I still managed the climb. Thank goodness it was more legs than hands to get up, but I was sweating by the time I reached the top.

She stared at my hand. "You really did hurt yourself. It's swollen. What did you do in the few minutes I was away?"

"I hit the wall." I walked past her. Where were we?

It was a broken hallway. The ceiling had come down a lot of places, not just on us. Where were my people? I looked left and right.

She put her hands on her hips. "Why did you hit the wall?"

"It needed hitting." I walked to where I thought my family would be. The floor moved slightly beneath me, and

I backed off. I didn't want to bring any more down on top of them. "There?"

She shook her head. "They're not there. If they're there, they're not alive. No heartbeats."

I swallowed. No. There wasn't a world without Chad, Deacon, Glen, and my father in it. I couldn't lose all of them *all* at once. "They got out."

"I hope so." She nodded.

At least she wasn't arguing. If I wanted to be in delusion about my family, then I could be. No, fuck it. I couldn't. I wouldn't leave their bodies down there to rot. I had to know one way or another. "We have to get down there."

"Right."

She had such a strange, twisted look on her face.

"What's wrong?"

"Of course we have to go down there and see. I mean, *of course* we do."

That didn't tell me anything. "And?"

"I almost asked if you wanted to find out about Icahn first. That thought startled me. Maybe I'm not human anymore. I mean, if I still had a family I'd want to know if they were alive. I'd want to… What is wrong with me? I'm not… human anymore. I must be some kind of sociopath and…"

I tugged her to me. "Okay, you had a shitty thought. I have them all the time. I broke my hand because I pounded on the wall thinking you'd taken off and left me to rot down there by myself. Nothing is as it should be anymore. The worst of humanity is constantly on display. You didn't ask it and you recognized the problem. Conscience. Doesn't that indicate you're not a sociopath?"

"I guess."

I couldn't believe I was having this conversation, but I

did like holding her in my arms. She fit there perfectly. "Do you feel sorry for me that my family might be dead down there?" Pain flared at the mere suggestion, but I suppressed it. Ruthless. I dealt in hypotheticals only. They weren't dead. Nope, not dead.

"I do. I feel awful. I also feel like we should move on this scientist thing."

Fine, she had a right to her reasons as she did to her secrets. Like my head suddenly getting better. But okay, I had some of my own, too.

I released her. Anxiety made my jaw tick. I had to do something, and I had to do it now. I ran a hand through my hair. She wanted to talk about the scientists now? Fuck. "Maybe you've been alone too long, or maybe you were always narcissistic and you're just figuring that out now."

I moved away from her. How was I going to get down there?

"Maybe I was."

I barely paid attention to her reply. I'd been kidding, sort of. I bent over and looked down. If they were dead, then it didn't matter if I brought down the ceiling. "No heartbeat?"

"None."

Okay. I bypassed her and picked up a piece of broken floor. It hurt my hand to hold it. I didn't care. Pain meant I was alive. I chucked the floor to the side. I did it again. And again. And again, until the floor gave out and a bigger hole opened. Rotted plaster and stone. That's all this was. How many hundreds of years had it stood until today? Why today of all days?

I stared down in the hall. It was dark save for the fluorescent lights illuminated from up here. Reminded of a conversation I'd had not too long ago—was it really only the day before?—I leapt down into the room. I was already broken. How much worse could it get?

"Micah," Brynna called to me. "Are you crazy?"

I nodded. "Yes."

There were no evidence of bodies, but there was a hole in the side wall someone had dug out. I let out a breath I'd held. No bodies and a way out, in the opposite direction of where I had been. They weren't dead. They were probably going for help to get to me. "They're not here. They got out."

"Okay, I'm jumping down."

She was what? "Be careful, I don't want you to hurt yourself."

"Well, I'd say catch me, big guy, but you broke your hand. I wouldn't want you to break the other one."

She landed steadier than I had. Brynna possessed an incredible grace about her. "Did you ever dance or something?"

"No." She walked past me toward the hole. "Guess we crawl? Should I assume we're not doing the stop Doctor Icahn from being re-cloned thing?"

Much as I admired how her ass looked in her pants while she poked her head through the hole, I wasn't going any farther until she and I shared some truth. "Why do you want to find him so badly? Before we brought it up, you were on a different mission. What is going on?"

"I think what I want and what you want are probably at the same place."

Now we were getting somewhere. "Which would be what?"

"The list of Vampires they think they could save. I want to find them. They have locations listed. They're guarding it like it's national secrets. Once I know the locations of Vampires who can be changed, I'll go find them. I will know who the Vampire is by name. It won't be Vampire in green, it'll be Hudson.

I supposed I followed her logic so far. "And then what?"

"And then I bring them to Margot, and she saves them."

I sighed. This was where she lost me. The doctor seemed fairly competent. She'd saved Deacon's life. But I didn't know about Vampire changing. Her family had held her captive. Why on earth would Brynna think Margot had answers? "You think Margot can do that?"

"If you think she can't, you're not paying close enough attention. She's a survivor like me. If she put her head down and pretended to not be the one who figured out how to save me, she's lying to you." She pointed at the hole. "I can't be the only one. There have to be others. She's going to fix them."

The idea that Margot had been feigning being simply an adequate doctor for months didn't sit well with me. I hated liars. Couldn't we all tell each other the truth for half a second?

"And when she saves the others, you're going to, what, ride off into the sunset as former Vamps, stopping to knock out unsuspecting humans or Wolves or whatever to feed off them when you're so compelled?"

Her gaze locked on me. I'd hit a nerve. Good, I'd been trying to. My dislike of liars extended to lying to myself. The last thing I wanted was her leaving with others like her. No idea why, but... fuck it. I didn't want her to leave with anyone.

She pointed at me. "You know what? Go screw yourself. I thought we could help each other. I thought maybe you were the nice guy I saw glimpses of and the one who made me..." Her voice trailed off. "Forget it. Find it yourself. But don't wait too long. The bogeyman Isaac Icahn might be coming. Guess what, Lyons, in terms of people out there to be afraid of? He's the least of your problems."

Brynna disappeared through the hole, vanishing in the blink of an eye. I sighed, and stared at the ground. *Why the hell do I do that?* If I wanted to keep embracing my policy of honesty, I had to be brutal. *I'm terrified about my family. Now she wants to leave. Then she tells me Margot has been lying to us, and I have to worry about her and the rest of damn Genesis.*

"Damn it." I crawled into the hole.

It wasn't a long crawl through the bricks. I emerged on the other side three minutes later. How had my family done this? Was one of them carrying a shovel? Probably Chad.

On the other side, I found an empty hallway. No sign of my family or Brynna. I sighed. That would be too easy. If I went left, I'd hit the entrance where the flashing lights had been, and right probably led to where Brynna went.

She was alone on this mission to find others like her. The people who were supposed to be like me had left together. I didn't even stop to think about what I planned to do next. My people were alive, but they didn't need me.

Brynna did.

Oh, who was I kidding? I needed her.

An angry moment couldn't be the last one between us. I wouldn't allow it, couldn't handle an argument being our goodbye.

I came to a fork in the hallway, and I sighed. Nothing was easy. If I went left, I'd hit the place where this all began, when Glen jumped down into the tech area. Brynna had been over there. I'd go that way until I found her. Even if I walked for weeks. My hand was broken, it hurt like hell and I...

I never saw what hit me, but I went down hard. Blackness rushed in all around me.

I came to briefly. I was on the floor somewhere. I tried to get to my feet, fast, and instead I tumbled backward.

"Do you have him?" asked a female voice I didn't know. The room spun, and two Vampire hands, pale, veiny, with long nails, grabbed me before I hit the floor.

I don't wish to hurt him. He belongs to her.

But the blood... they'll take away the blood....

I didn't know whose voice it was, and I didn't care. I'd had two serious head blows, and I was out for the count.

In my dream, I walked the streets of New York. They were empty. No traffic. No cars. Just the sound of babies crying. Everywhere.

Chapter 6

Two Vampires stood over me. This had to be some kind of nightmare, except I was awake. They'd strapped me to a medical table. Bandages covered my arm. What in the hell was happening? I struggled to breathe, my chest tight like I was having an asthma attack. I'd grown out of them when I was eight. But I'd never forgotten this feeling. I couldn't defend myself from these two. Whoever had knocked me out had left me here to be easy prey.

Well… I supposed it had been a hell of a good run. I was only sorry I couldn't apologize to Brynna for being a dipshit.

"Ivan?" That was the only name I knew. The one she'd spoken to in the hallway, she'd called him Ivan. It was kind of a perfect name for a Vampire. "You can't both be Ivan."

The pair made eye contact then studied me. These were pretty with it Vampires, didn't seem particularly out of it at all.

Okay, take two. "Brynna really liked my blood. Glad to know I'll be an enjoyable last meal."

The sound of footsteps behind me had both Vampires turning their attention. They retreated a step, and Brynna appeared in my vision. "Micah. What in the world happened?"

I shook my head. "Don't they know?" The two Vampires abandoned their lurking, gliding away from us.

She sighed. "You're lucky they had control of the bloodlust." She undid my straps. "I started seeing you like this moving through memories. I came looking."

I tried to sit up, and she had to help me. Wow, I was weak. "I was trying to find you."

"I was trying to find you, too. Turns out I care about what happens to you even if you're an asshole."

I let her guide me off the table. They'd clearly gone to town pricking me with needles while I'd been out of it. What had they done to me? "I am an asshole. I care about what happens to you, too."

I had to lean on her, which was humiliating. "What did they do to me?"

"They poked you a lot. The Vampires don't know more than that. Apparently, the scientists were looking for you. Come on. We need to get you out of here before they return. It's quite a walk."

Nope, I wasn't going to make it. "Deposit me in a corner somewhere. Get yourself out before they find you."

She huffed. "That's not happening. If you're not strong enough to get out of here yet, we'll go somewhere closer. Keep walking as best you can, one foot in front of the other. Lean on me."

I did the best I could. Speaking proved to be too much, so I made my way with her and concentrated on not falling over. The last of us to encounter a scientist had been Deacon. They'd given him a horrible drug that nearly killed him. Was that what they did to me? I didn't feel bad, only weak.

Eventually, we found a small room with a sleeping pad in the corner. "Is this where you've been staying?" I could barely say the words.

"Yes." She helped me down on the pad. "If it means anything, in the memories, it seemed more like they took blood. They didn't inject you with medication."

It did. I crawled onto the pad. She knelt down next to me before she kissed my cheek. "You're going to be okay, asshole."

I loved how she put things.

———

I WOKE up some time later with no idea how long I'd been out. I could tell it had been a long haul, because I was stiff everywhere. There was only a touch of light coming through the bottom of the door, keeping it from pitch darkness. So this is where she slept when she was here. Of course, where else did she go? I didn't know much about her, although I wanted to.

Where was she? "Brynna?"

"I'm here." She was across the room. "I can't go near you right now."

Well… that sucked. "Why? Do I smell? I'm sure I need to shower. I…"

She laughed. "No. I wish it was so simple. Suddenly, I have to feed again. I don't know why. It should have been a month. I don't understand, and you are obviously not in any condition to…"

Oh but fuck did I suddenly want it. It didn't make any sense to me either. "I'm not sure I have enough to give." I stumbled to my feet. "I love the idea, too."

"Let's get you out of here. I'm going to stay a distance ahead of you. I don't want to go far. But I'm not sure I can resist biting you, which is all kinds of wrong. I know."

I stayed where I was and waited for her to move in front of me. "What's happening to us, Brynna?"

"I don't know."

That didn't sound encouraging.

IT TOOK me twice as long to get out as it should have, but at least I was steadier than when I first got out of the scientist's med bay. My hand still throbbed. The doctors had clearly not thought to fix it when they had me on the table. I climbed slowly up the ladder until finally we made it above ground. The sun burned my eyes, and I almost slipped down a rung.

Brynna grabbed my arm and steadied me. "Easy there, killer."

"You come up with the greatest names for me."

She laughed, and I waited for my eyes to adjust.

Brynna touched the side of my face. "You look like shit."

"Yeah, I bet I do." I could only imagine. "Everything hurts. I might be down for the count for a little bit, which is highly unusual for me. I took down a bunch of Werewolves when I had the flu."

Brynna breathed heavily. I'd never seen her in daylight. She was even lovelier. Her dark hair had a lot more colors in it than I'd seen before. Red and blonde streaks. Her eyes were multicolored, too. Fuck, she was beautiful.

I already knew, but it was like I was seeing it for the first time again.

"I want to fix you, so badly." She put her hands on my arms.

I shook my head. "I thought you didn't have magical Vampire healing abilities."

"I don't. And that's why I can't understand this." She stepped back. "I can't bite you. There is hardly any blood left in you. I can hear your body struggling. Let's get you back to Margot. I'll take you as far as I can, and then I'll…"

"No." I didn't like where this was going. "You're going to stay with me. For a little bit anyway."

The idea of us separating ignited a sense of panic. Fear crawled up my spine. I had to bite my tongue to keep from saying something nasty, a knee-jerk reaction to terror.

I glued my lips together. I'd keep my mouth shut. Nothing would be better than something awful.

"Micah!" Chad's shout from a distance broke up the moment.

Brynna caught her breath and looked away. "Your people are here."

"Sometimes they feel like my people, and sometimes they don't." I couldn't take my gaze off of her. If I did, she might not know. I didn't know what it was exactly she might not *know*, but she might not *know* it. Damn, I was losing my mind.

She gave me a small smile. "They're your people. Don't forget that. I'm going to take care of your scientist problem. Stay up here in the sunlight. Leave the darkness for the monsters."

"Brynna…"

I reached for her, but she was gone. That fast. I fell forward, my knees giving out. Chad was there to catch me before I hit the ground. If I'd had any ability left to care, I might have found that humiliating.

MARGOT LISTENED TO MY HEARTBEAT, checked my blood pressure, and still hadn't said anything about what I'd told her. We weren't alone. Apparently, every Warrior in Genesis had gotten ready to come rescue me, and since I officially didn't need rescuing, they prowled the area of my doctor's appointment.

In the end, my father, Chad, and Deacon were all with me.

"Explain." My dad was apparently sick of waiting. "He was concussed. He… had sex with her, she bit him, and now he's not concussed. Then whatever the scientists did to him, the broken hand… explain it to me."

I supposed I should have kept some of those events to myself. I didn't really want to talk about having sex with Brynna in front of my father. But I needed answers, and the leader of Genesis learned anything pertaining to the Vampires. If there was some magical healing thing, he had to hear about it.

So much for the years of privacy…

Margot crossed her arms. "I can speculate. I don't have the equipment I need here to really know."

"Good enough," I answered before anyone else could. Chad inserted himself between my father and me. I wondered if we were about to have a fight. I didn't have the energy to care.

She sighed. "One of the things done to Brynna to cure her from Vampirism was that we infused her with some Werewolf DNA. The Werewolves couldn't become Vampires. It worked."

I waited for her to continue. "Was I supposed to understand something from Werewolf DNA? Congratulations on finding something that worked, but what the hell does that mean for me?"

Margot looked down. "Werewolves can heal their mates. The blood exchange in the mating process gives the mate increased healing. I think the fact she bit you and *then* kissed you may have allowed you to exchange blood. Maybe it's saliva entering the wound when she bit you. Could be that easy. I don't know. The DNA change in her might have given her some of those properties."

"Oh, well that's good, then. We had our moment and…"

She put her hand on my arm and stopped me. "Micah, are you missing her? I know you're not feeling well. We have to splint up your hand, and you've had some serious blood loss. Rest. Fluids. Iron. Okay. But you're jumpy. Usually, you're so mellow I'm not sure if you're awake."

My father snorted. "That's just because he wasn't hitting on you."

I got up on my knees on the table, reached around Chad, and yanked my father toward me by the shirt. He needed to know I was deadly serious. "Those days are behind me. Do you understand?"

Chad restrained our father while Deacon took my hands off Dad's shirt. I breathed hard. I was sore, exhausted, and slightly broken, but I wasn't afraid. If it came to this, it came to this.

"Micah," Chad yelled at me. "Not okay with what he said, but shit, man."

"I…"

Margot stepped into the fray. "Everyone stop. This is mate behavior. He can't help it."

Wait. "What?"

Margot sighed. "If Brynna's small amount of DNA has given her this ability to heal, then it's possible it also gave her some of the other aspects of being a Werewolf. Okay? They mate. It's a binding. I don't know every detail of your... exchange with Brynna, but the way you are feeling is how mates feel when they separate from their other half."

None of this made any sense. "I'm mated? Wait. No. Okay?" I had to be sensible and not lose my mind before I understood what she was saying. "Jason, he was a Werewolf who's dead now, he always said he was mated to Rachel. She didn't miss him like this when he wasn't around."

Margot nodded. "Look, I only studied them from a distance."

Chad looked away. "So screwed up you were studying any of this at all. Be careful what you say here, we're talking about my wife."

"I wasn't going to say anything bad, Chad. Jason, Rachel, they were test studies to me. I'm sorry that upsets you. It bothers me, too. I read a lot about them. And I've come to believe Rachel was not really Jason's mate."

My brother's eyebrows rose. "She's human. He felt it. She didn't."

"Doesn't work that way. Jason's mother was human. She and his father were truly mated. The human feels the mating. They just do. Could be they never had sex, Rachel and Jason, presuming they didn't. That wouldn't have mattered either. He was fixated with her, but it wasn't mating. Maybe he wanted it to be. That's why Andon kept trying to get rid of Rachel. He knew it wasn't true either." She shook her head. "You, by contrast, Micah, are mated. If it means anything, you had to have wanted her for this to have happened. Something about the two of you connected."

My father, having found his voice again, used it. "Of

course he is. Leave it to Micah to mate the fucking monster."

I attacked him.

———

CHAD STARED at me after dumping me on the bed in my tent. My hand was in a splint, an icepack on my eye since my father had a pretty good left hook, and I was all around more sore than I had even been earlier. I'd gotten in a few blows of my own but not nearly enough to satisfy me.

"Don't say it."

He squatted in front of my bed. "Not going to. What are you going to do?"

"What is there to do?" I rolled onto my side. "I have to find her. Like I have to do it as though it's the only way I can keep breathing. That's the mating thing. I get it. And yet, I'm not able to do anything about it, and I'm not sure I would if I could. But maybe I only feel this way because of the mating."

Chad rose, patting my foot. "You know where we are if you need us."

"It's like I can't think because I don't know where she is or if she's okay."

He rubbed his chin. "Start by assuming she is. We'll figure this out. You're going to get through this."

For once, I was pretty sure Chad had no idea what he was talking about.

After he left, I tossed and turned. I had to talk to Margot, let her know I knew she was full of shit and if she hurt Genesis in any way, she'd know the wrath of me. That type of conversation wouldn't go well if I was this weak.

I rubbed my eyes. I had to find Brynna. I threw my legs over the side of the bed. Okay, she was like a drug, and I was an addict. Fine, I needed my fix. I'd figure out how to...

"Micah." Brynna came through the door. I jolted. How had she gotten here? Damn, I didn't care. I'd get details later. She was quickly by my side in a second. "I don't know what's going on. I shouldn't be here. I'm not fit to be around people. But I can't stay away."

I held out my hand. I had to touch her. "There's a reason for that." I sighed. "Margot has an explanation. Apparently, to make a long story short, they saved you with Werewolf DNA. So what we have done is, ah, mated. Sorry about that."

She rose to her feet. "What?"

"Do you want me to explain it again? I..."

Brynna shook her head. "I'm going to find Margot."

Just like that, she was gone.

I fell back on the bed. Knowing she was okay did settle me down a little bit. I groaned. This was all my fault. I went down below when I should have stayed where I was, helping Genesis, but I always had to push and push. Now this had happened, and Brynna was stuck with me.

The tent flap opened with a whoosh. I sighed. "That was fast."

"Micah?" I lifted my head. This person wasn't Brynna, but a higher-pitched, whinier voice.

"Who's there?" I couldn't see in the dark. I had to light one of my lanterns or latch my flap to allow better illumination.

The unknown woman walked toward me. "I heard you were back."

Sadly, the truth was I had no idea who this person was, let alone why she'd be at all interested in the fact I was back. "Who are you?"

"Oh." She twirled the end of her hair. Was it blonde?

Brown? "I guess you don't remember me, but I'll never forget you. My name is Marilyn. I thought maybe I could make you feel better like you made me feel better months ago. I haven't been able to stop thinking of you."

I didn't know who she was. Maybe someone else would be proud of having had some kind of encounter they couldn't quite recall, but not me. Shame at how little I cared about the people who shared my bed for an evening.

My mother would be ashamed and right to be. I'd been raised to have more respect than I had been showing women.

"Marilyn, look." I tried to get up. "I'm not sure what you thought was going to happen here." I managed to get to my feet. "But it's…"

She touched my arm, and I stepped back. I really didn't want her touching me. I stumbled back onto the bed.

"I can make you feel better, Micah."

I shook my head. "No, thank you. You should go."

She grabbed both my arms. "You know I can make you feel good."

I remembered Marilyn right then. She had been… persistent on a night when I'd intended to go home alone. I'd ended up figuring oh what the hell and taken her back to her tent for a couple of hours together. She'd told me later she was in an on again off again relationship with someone named Eric who worked in non-Warrior security.

They'd been on the off part of that relationship, and since she was certainly not thinking about him tonight, they must still be in that off zone.

"Marilyn, I'm involved with someone. Okay? I'm not free. Please, stop. Just go." I realized as I said it, I meant it. I was, at least at present, mated to Brynna, and I wasn't at all interested in this extremely willing woman in front of me.

The air moved in the way it did whenever Brynna arrived anywhere. The slightest change in the atmosphere when she was near.

"I think he told you to go." Her voice sounded low, different than I was used to hearing. She moved slowly, almost gliding. I knew that look. I'd seen it night after night with the Vampires.

I took a deep breath. She didn't like Marilyn in here anymore than I did. The only difference was Brynna had fangs. I pushed the unwanted Marilyn behind me. "She was leaving."

"Oh, I don't think so." Brynna tilted her head to the side. "She means to have you."

I grabbed Marilyn with the wrong hand and hissed out a breath. Damn, I'd had less trouble dealing with being stabbed in the abdomen than remembering to not use my bad hand. "She can mean anything she wants. She's leaving."

I dragged-slash-helped Marilyn out of my tent before I whirled around to face Brynna. "She's gone."

She flared her nostrils. "Micah, I want to kill her. I want to drain her blood until her eyes go blank."

Wow. *Okay.* "There's no need. I get it. Whatever has happened here between us has made us attached. I'd want to kill a man for getting near you right now. You need to know nothing was going to happen, period. Until we can figure out how to get you separated from me so you can go on with your life, we're both going to act like the taken people we are. Deal?"

She put her hands on her hips. "Micah, I think in this scenario, you are likely the one who is stuck. Margot was less than helpful. I know she can fix us like I know she can fix the other Vampires. Yet, she's over there insisting to me she can't." Brynna looked down at the ground. "You're in pain."

"Aw now, honey, I've been in pain before." I went for flirty. Hopefully, it would defuse some of her anger. A mad, out of control Brynna wasn't going to be good for anyone. "And you don't know me well enough yet. Trust me, former Vampire with Werewolf DNA, I still got the better end of this deal."

She jumped me. I didn't see it coming, and we both fell back on the bed. Heat rushed inside of me, and I was instantly hard. Brynna kissed me. The time for talking was gone.

I PULLED her against my side tighter. She was awake, but weaker than I had known her, and considering she'd sampled my blood quite a bit, she should have been feeling stronger. "You okay?"

She nodded. "Sated."

Good word choice. I'd take it. My hand was fixed. In fact, every ache in my body seemed to be gone. I yawned. "Do you suppose we can have sex without me being injured sometime?"

"How about in the morning? Can you manage to not get hurt between now and then?"

Yeah, I supposed I could. "Sure. Want to talk or sleep?"

She rolled her eyes at me. "As you are talking, I am probably not going to sleep." She paused for a second. "Micah, I'm sorry about all of this. I was going to kill that girl. I am so glad you got her out of here when you did. And this is my fault. All of it. I was attracted to you. Obviously, everyone is. The difference being I bound you to me."

"I'm not upset about it." That didn't make a lot of sense, but it was true. "Maybe it's a mating thing. I feel pretty fine with things today."

She shook her head. "That's just your body getting adjusted to this new… thing between us. I can feel it, too. You didn't choose it. I'm not going to be what you got stuck with. We'll figure out how to get rid of this."

I hated the idea of losing her. Still, she was probably right that my general lack of anger about this had to do with the fact we were now linked or whatever. "Well, I guess we're going back down tomorrow to find out things from those scientists."

"Sounds like a plan." She drummed her fingers on me. "All of the scenes I've seen over the years in memories and my own minimal experience, I have to say this is the strangest post-coital conversation I've ever witnessed."

I leaned up on my elbow. "So is it like the Borg?"

She blinked. "Star Trek?"

Had she watched it? I used to stay up all night, watching it on the Sci-Fi channel in reruns. "Yes."

"I've seen it through others' memories. Um, yes. I guess it's like the Borg, sort of. It's more like touches of every other Vampire's memories eventually move through my mind. I can't touch it like I used to. Only if it is specifically designated to me. Like they're making me see on purpose. That's what they did when you were in the Med Bay. It moved from them to others, but they were all trying to reach me. It used to be more universal."

I wasn't sure I'd ever understand, but I'd go with Borg. My limited intellect could only handle so much "We'd never have known each other. If Icahn and the others didn't take over the world. Isn't that weird to think about."

"Oh, we might have. I mean, eventually I'd have been in graduate school. You'd have come to New York City, maybe for Fleet Week. You'd have been in that uniform…"

I liked her imagery, so I let her tell me the fairy tale about how we might have met. It was better than listening to the sounds of the Werewolves outside.

Chapter 7

I woke up in the morning feeling better than I had in days. Brynna lived up to her promise and made love to me even though I wasn't hurt. She sucked my blood from the spot on my neck we both liked, and I came inside of her, hard. I hadn't used a condom with her, and while I wasn't worried about protecting myself, the guilt of knowing I might have left her pregnant seeped into my general feeling of post-sex bliss.

I kissed her temple. "Brynna, we have totally taken no precautions. This is all on me. Do you want to go see Margot?"

She shook her head. "Not fertile. I haven't had a period since I came back to myself and stopped wanting to kill everyone."

Well, that was good. We took our time getting out of bed, and I watched as she dressed. Brynna was everything I loved about women. The curves. The long lines. The graceful movements. The way she was small yet strong.

I tugged on my shirt and had the benefit of seeing her blush at my admiration. We were heading back down to get to the scientists. This easy morning wouldn't last long. I intended to enjoy every second of it.

We'd left the tent and were headed back to the underground entrance when Deacon's shout stopped me from going any further. I turned to see my best friend and his wife running toward us.

"Do you need help? Lydia and I can sneak away." Deacon panted. We all had to work on our cardio. This was getting ridiculous. Sometimes, we had to run for our lives.

Brynna went stiff beside me. I glanced at her and then Deacon. "No, you're in charge now. You can't go sneaking off."

I smiled at Lydia. She had been just what Deacon always needed but hadn't known he'd needed. "I think we're okay. Lydia, have you met Brynna. Brynna, Lydia."

My mate—and it was weird to think that—extended her hand, and Lydia shook it. "Hello," Lydia remarked and Brynna returned. I didn't know what was going on, but there was tension.

"Deacon," Brynna finally said, "it's so nice of you to offer to help us. I wouldn't think you would want to be anywhere near me."

Why? I turned to ask her when a memory hit me. It was what Brynna described. I suddenly picked up a vision —a memory—as though it floated through the air to reach me. I saw Deacon. He was a baby, yet I knew it was him. He rolled a truck to another toddler and laughed. It must have been Brynna's eyes I viewed this through. She was so unbelievably sad. Bad things happened in the world. She couldn't save anyone from the bloodlust when it came. Inside her mind, she screamed at the top of her lungs.

I blinked, and I was back in my body. My heart raced. How did Brynna live with memories like that? How many did she hold on to with so much guilt? I turned to her, uncaring if Deacon and Lydia were present. "It's not like you could control it."

She visibly swallowed. "I wanted to. I wanted to die, okay? I'd have done anything not to be a Vampire."

Deacon looked between us. "Look, since I've had time to sit with the idea you're sick, that people who are Vampires are sick, I've had some time to consider none of it was any of your fault."

"That's very big of you, Deacon. I blame myself for a lot of it. See, the thing is, I don't really remember becoming a Vampire. I wasn't. Then I was. I have this vague recollection of news reports. I don't know what happened to my family. They're not in Vampire memories, so they're dead not changed."

I shook my head to Deacon. I wasn't going to explain what she meant right then. She continued. "I was one of the beings that hurt all of you. There's no making up for it. Even if I wasn't really me during that time. I can remember it. I'm sorry."

Lydia put her hand on Deacon's arm. "You saying you're sorry and giving us a sense of things is more than we expected. It's okay, Brynna. You're forgiven."

"No." She shook her head. "I never will be."

Her pain was my own, and all I wanted was to get her away from it. "Thanks, guys. We're going to go."

How much could she blame herself? I wasn't in her head. I couldn't know how much she could have prevented, if anything. All I knew was the past was past. She was as much a victim in this as the rest of us.

I held her hand tightly, and we didn't speak until we got to the hole. I stared at her. "What was it like to need to feed like that? The bloodlust?"

"All encompassing." She didn't hesitate. "It was like I

was always lost in a wave of memories, they weren't a bad place to be, and then you're rushed back into your head. You have a few minutes of clarity, to know who you are, where you are, *what* you are, and what you've been doing in the time you've been lost to reality. Somehow, your body did things while you weren't conscious, and then boom! The bloodlust hits and suddenly you have to get your hit of the blood, and it has to be the stuff with the addictive properties in it, that the scientists see to it that all humans have one way or another, and you're running through the dark. Conscious, aware, and out of control."

Well… didn't that sound like a special kind of hell?

Chapter 8

We didn't encounter anyone this time. Lights flashed on and off in rapid succession. A nagging headache clung behind my eyes. I didn't care. We had to do this, and I was sick and tired of getting waylaid.

The scientists hung out in an area of the underground, that turned out to be quite a distance to travel. Brynna and I didn't speak much, and I couldn't say it was because I was lost in my own thoughts. The truth was there was so much to think about that I really didn't find myself able to focus on anything. I'd get waves of clarity on a subject, and then boom, it was gone. *I was mated...* and then whatever I'd wanted to say would float right out of my head. Maybe it was exhaustion, or maybe there was simply nothing more to think about.

Brynna dropped my hand, and I almost snatched it back like a lunatic. Instead, I managed to resist the urge and kept walking. Seconds later, she linked our hands again. "I thought maybe you were getting tired of holding it."

I tried not to smile and maybe looked deranged with the effort. "If I was sick of holding it, I'd let you know."

"I… Do you think this is going to get worse? The need for each other? Or better? Oh, it doesn't matter. We're fixing it anyway."

She tugged me in the direction she wanted to go, and I didn't object. She knew our destination and the area, whereas I didn't. Besides, her words irked me, and it was ridiculous. That was the thing with my long term issues, I had very little control when it came to dealing with them. In the old days, I could probably have used a good long dose of talk therapy. The sickest part of the whole thing—I recognized abandonment and feeling unwanted were huge triggers for me, and the knowledge didn't free me at all.

"So when it comes to this mating with me, is it the mating you object to in general or being stuck with me specifically?" There. I'd asked the question in a nice, rational manner. I hadn't yelled or insulted her. Go me.

Brynna stopped. She raised one eyebrow. It was kind of a sexy, angry look on her. "You can't be serious."

I didn't follow her statement. "About what?"

"You can't in any world want to be stuck here with me in this mating. You're Micah Lyons. You don't have one girl, you have hundreds."

A muscle ticked in my jaw. It felt like a jolt of electricity moved from my cheek up my head. So much for my earlier success. "That's what you think? That I'm going to just go fuck someone else? That's what you think of me. Okay, good to know."

She dropped my hand, which was good. I was about to tell her I was sick of holding it, which would be a damned lie, but I'd say it anyway. Forget my issue with lying. I'd live with the guilt.

"Micah, you're not being reasonable. You don't want to commit to me."

I leaned over until our foreheads touched. "What's clear to me is you don't. That's fine. We'll get ourselves unmated, and you can get on with being holier than thou or whatever it is you do with your time."

She gasped, and I left her behind as I stormed through the door into what had to be a working lab. All right, at last we were getting somewhere. There weren't any humans around, which was both good and bad. We could search without having to fight anyone, but it also meant they weren't actively using this area and, therefore, it could be a huge waste of time.

Brynna was suddenly right by my side. I'd almost gotten used to her moving like that. "Days ago, you were calling me a monster."

"You asked me not to, and I said I wouldn't anymore." I walked over to an old looking computer. "They don't seriously use this stuff? This tech was old when we were living in the correct timeline."

She sighed loudly. "Are you going to just end this conversation?"

This was so typical. "You'd fit right in with my family. Criticize me, say shitty things, get angry when I respond and passive aggressive when I want to move on."

She pointed her finger at me. "There is nothing about how I am feeling that is passive, Micah, and I am not your family. You would never have actively chosen this, and neither would I. So get over yourself."

Yep, she'd fit right the fuck in. And if she was correct, too, then what else was new? We searched in silence. I pulled every file that said Vampire cure, and she managed to get the old computer working. As if to answer my much earlier statement, she talked about the computer. "You can't keep massive tech working without infrastructure. Old computers proved sturdier than the newer stuff. Back when they made things not to break."

I almost asked her how she knew. Then it hit me, she saw memories. Someone who knew this stuff had become a Vampire, and now she knew it, too.

I scowled. There was nothing I'd run across that said mating. I bet this stuff was old. I took the files and set them aside on a medical table, then headed into a second room.

After I flipped on the lights, I stopped abruptly. Across the room sat a cloning machine. Brynna had said there were a ton of them. I almost called to her and then rethought it. She was busy, and I was... raw. Even if I was being manipulated by the mating, the last thing I needed was another person in my life who'd prefer I wasn't around.

I walked to the machine and stared at it. A green light indicated it was on and had a power source. I touched the cool metal, as if it might reveal its secrets to me. A sister to this device was the reason my brother lived and breathed. What might they have done with something like this back in the early days if they'd used it to help people instead of control them? Throat cancer? No problem, they'd grow you a new one and replace the one you had. Why hadn't these geniuses with unfathomable minds done helpful things?

I wasn't smart, and even I knew there had to be better purposes for this kind of innovation than what they'd done with it.

Behind the cloning machine was an empty tank that looked like it should have been filled with water, like at an aquarium. I tapped the glass.

I really was wasting time. We had to move on from here and find more useful stuff. I wasn't cut out for this. Killing Vampires? Yes. Making sense of science? Not so much.

The cloning machine seemed harmless. I pressed the up button on the device to scan up. The monitor showed a jumble of numbers and letters. Twelve letters to be exact, written with small changes in each sequence. AAGC-TAGCTAGC. What was this? I didn't know, but I kept scanning through.

Brynna's voice was tight. "Do you think it's a good idea to be touching the cloning machine?"

I shrugged. "I'm not going to hit anything that could cause a problem. I'm only looking. None of it makes sense. Mostly letters, numbers here and there. I think this one is broken. When we broke the cloning machines Icahn was using, he had big tanks filled with water in the room. This one is empty."

"Fair enough. I don't know how to work it." She strolled toward me. "None of the scientists who worked on this mess have ever been made Vampires."

"And doesn't that speak volumes to the bullshit of this entire thing." I stepped away from the machine.

My body went cold, and I doubled over. I knew the sign. "Werewolf. More than one."

She whirled around. "I don't hear it."

"Doesn't matter. It's here."

A roar sounded in the hallway a moment before two shifted Werewolves charged into the room. I found my strength the way I'd been taught—I dug deep for it—and I shoved Brynna behind me. She might have been fast, but she wasn't a fighter. This was my job. I wrenched the machete off my back.

These were trained Wolves. They knew how to fight Warriors. Lately, they'd gotten better. I whirled around, grabbing a chair and throwing it at one while I swinging my machete through the neck of the other. It took two strokes, but I got the head off.

"Brynna, run. I can't worry about you and do this."

She didn't argue which I appreciated. I faced down the other Werewolf. To the one side of me, the machine I'd been looking at made a strange noise as though it powered up. The chair I'd thrown landed on top of it after it hit the Werewolf.

Fine. I'd deal with whatever was happening after. The beast and I circled each other slowly. He growled and leapt at me, which was his first mistake. The Werewolves always gave in to the aggression or more of them would beat us. It was a dominance struggle. If he waited me out, he seemed weaker.

He jumped, I struck.

His head rolled to the side. Victorious, I spoke to the dead Wolf. "I wait you guys out every time. One of you should have killed me by now."

Brynna appeared by my side and threw her arms around me. "I didn't leave. I didn't want to distract you."

She smelled like roses. I whistled against her shoulder. "I told you to go."

"I don't listen really well, and the thing you said to me before? I'm sorry if I made you feel those things; I'm sorry if you feel unwanted. I don't want either of us to be stuck. If you want me, after we fix this, that's a different story."

I didn't want to think about any of that. The buzzing of the cloning machine reached my ears, and I let go of Brynna to go see what was happening. Red and yellow lights blinked, and the once empty tank was filling with water. I hit what looked like the power button, and it didn't shut off. Brynna gasped.

"Did we accidently turn this thing on and tell it to clone someone?"

I appreciated the *we*, but she hadn't done any of that. I did. Or at least, I was the one who had thrown the chair that hit the fucking thing. "Is there a plug?"

She shook her head. "Look, I don't know much about this at all. But the memories the few Vampires had who have been in here when this happened seem to indicate once the process starts, it can't be stopped."

"Well, who are we cloning because so help me, if I have brought back Icahn, I am never going to hear the end of it, trust me. I'm going to wait here and kill him before he can do whatever he'll do."

Brynna tugged on my arm. "I don't think we have that kind of time. They'll know this is on now. They'll come in droves. I'll never be able to stop the Vampires they have with them from killing us."

"Will they come after us or just if the scientists see us?" I didn't give her time to answer. Instead, I ran into the other room and grabbed an empty trunk. It was huge, and I bet at one time, it had held all sorts of medical equipment. "Go from here, Brynna. Take yourself somewhere safe. I'll be fine. Just, go. Besides, if something happens to me, you'll be free from this mess."

She huffed. "That's not funny, Micah."

"Good. I wasn't joking." I jumped into the trunk. One way or another, I was going to see who was coming out of the cloning machine. "Go, Brynna. Now."

Instead, she pushed her way in. The trunk was big enough for me to feel solidly uncomfortable in it. With the addition of Brynna, we were achingly cramped. That was okay. Sounds of running footsteps stopped me from arguing. I closed the trunk, sticking my finger in it to stop it from closing all the way. With the tiniest spot to look through, I'd get my answers.

I hoped no one thought to see why the trunk wasn't where they had left it.

Brynna was right. The room was suddenly filled with people wearing white lab coats—twelve of them.

A female voice spoke. "We need to get the feed in here hooked back up. We can't be caught unaware. We didn't think the Wolves would figure out the machine, but it looks like they did."

The Wolves? They'd been present, come when he touched the machine. Why were they interested in cloning? This was all so confusing. If there were so many cloning machines, why had Icahn been overly upset when Rachel broke his?

These were questions for Margot, ones I intended to get the answers to when I got out of this trunk.

"Everything is broken. With Icahn back, we can go see Doubleday. She'll talk to us now. Then we'll get things working again. I'm tired of living in this hellhole. This wasn't what was promised," a man answered.

Someone groaned. "They brought back the Kenwood boy. I guess those furry assholes really can't live without their leadership. They wanted an Alpha, they made one. What do you want me to do? Kill it when it wakes up? And look those Warriors must have chased them in and killed some of them. This place is such a mess. I want a transfer. I hate this quadrant."

"Don't kill it. They'll simply bring it back again. What I want is to destroy this machine altogether, but Doubleday won't hear of it." The man speaking sighed. "I say we let the guy show up. Looks like they aged him. Fuck. They've really been paying attention to this. It'll be the perfect age to go after the Clancy bitch again. Or Lyons or whatever. Maybe he'll kill her this time when he succumbs. Let's not feed him when he wakes up. He can be hungry and confused."

My heart rate kicked up. Jason Kenwood was coming back, and they hoped he killed my sister-in-law. I'd done this. I closed my eyes. Icahn was back, so there was no stopping his cloning. I was mated to a woman who used to be a Vampire who didn't want me.

I was one big mess of trouble everywhere I went.

———

RAIN POUNDED ON MY HEAD. I didn't care. Jason Kenwood was coming back. Isaac Icahn had *already* returned. Why did I ever think I could fix anything? I stood on top of the hill staring at Genesis, and I didn't give one single fuck about the freezing rain soaking through my clothes. I turned to Brynna. "You should go," I called over the noise. "They're going to come down on me like a ton of bricks. I really don't know what's going to happen."

"Then better to not leave you." If the rain bothered her, she didn't indicate. Still, I'd rather she not get any wetter than she already was.

"Brynna, you're going to catch your death." I sounded like my grandmother. For the first time in forever, I missed her.

An old memory moved through me, catching me by surprise. Nana wasn't a pretty woman by any means. I didn't think she'd ever been. But she loved my grandfather with abandon and thought her son, my father, walked on water. Consequently, we all did. She laughed, holding my six-year-old self against her while she stirred her tea.

"Micah, you come from sturdy stuff." She kissed my

cheek, and she smelled like tomatoes. The woman had made the best sauce. "We sometimes falter, but we never fail. Not when it comes down to it. Your great-grandfather was a prince, and you have his name."

My father would later tell me her stories were all made up. My family had come over to the United States in lieu of being executed for stealing. They'd then been indentured servants for years before gaining their freedom. I smirked. I liked her version better.

I blinked back into the here and now. Thinking of someone was dangerous around Brynna.

"She loved you."

"She did. She might be the last person to have really done so."

I was glad to have her memory at the front of my mind. My father, I would later realize when I was finally able to see adults for what they were—people, instead of gods—was embarrassed by his mother. She chewed with her mouth open. She spoke too loud. He hadn't cared that every time she made dinner she'd done so with love. He hadn't remembered she'd sat up nights sewing his socks so he never had holes even when he was an adult. My mother would bring her the socks. I cringed. I'd forgotten my grandmother, too. She doctored my skinned knees. She never overlooked me for Chad or disregarded Chad for me. Tia wasn't better because she was a girl. We were all the same.

She'd died when I was ten, and everyone had moved on like the next day was normal. I'd had to force myself to only weep in the bathroom when no one could hear.

"People love you, Micah."

I pinched my lips. "Chad loves me. But he has her heart. Our grandmother. I realize it now. My dad and I... we're two of a kind. And I get to go tell the people down there that their lives are about to get much, much worse. Not sure even my pretty face or my last name will matter now." I winked at her. When in doubt, flirt. "It's been nice knowing you, Brynna. Good luck with everything."

I walked toward my destiny. Somehow, it had always been moving toward this.

Chapter 9

I missed Brynna the second I left her, but I had to ignore the ache. I searched until I found Deacon. He was home with his wife. She had her feet up while he rubbed them. I could see through the makeshift windows in the tent. Lydia laughed at something he said. I was too wet to go inside. I'd get water everywhere, and unlike my home, they'd actually taken the time with theirs to make it look like someplace a person would want to spend time.

I knocked on the window until they both looked at me. Yeah, they could both call me Peeping Micah. I was pressed against their window like a creeper.

Deacon opened the door flap and stuck his head out. "Hey, man, come inside."

"No." I shook my head. "I can't." I wouldn't be welcome anymore in anyone's home. I'd officially cloned a Werewolf that had tried to kill us all, and I didn't have the balls to stay there and kill him. As soon as I could, I'd run away. Because I was a coward on top of everything else.

Deacon stepped outside into the rain. I hadn't wanted

him to do that. I'd only wanted to tell him what I knew. "Go back out of the storm."

"Why can't you come in?" He stayed by the door. I stepped away from the window. I wouldn't spy on him anymore.

"Because you won't want me in there."

Deacon scrunched up his nose. "Why?"

"I'm a coward, and you never are." I spoke the truth. It felt good to do so. "I cloned Jason Kenwood. I didn't mean to, but I did. Because, fuck, that's what I do, right? I fuck up. Icahn is already back. And there's somebody named Doubleday who's actually running the show. You want to get your raincoat or umbrella or whatever the fuck you want and go get my father. Someone needs to arrest me. I'll stay here."

Deacon didn't do as I asked. In fact, he made no noticeable movements. He lifted his eyebrows. That was all.

"Micah," Brynna called to me, and I turned to the left to see her standing there. "Chad doesn't have her heart. You do." I almost couldn't breathe after she spoke her words. The storm picked up, the rain flying sideways at us. "Your grandmother. I can see her in your head—I don't know how this memory sharing works—and I can see her in Chad's. You have her heart. Your father wasn't nice enough to her. Chad knew, knows, whatever, that, too. But you have her heart. They haven't taken good enough care of it. You are not your father. Tia is maybe the closest, but I don't know her. I haven't met her. All I know is you have it. You love like she did. Completely. Without reservation. The only difference is she had your grandfather, until he died. And he loved her the right way. That's how she got through all of it, I think. That's what Chad thought. That's what she told him, once."

I felt like a voyeur for the second time in minutes. First I was looking through Deacon's window and now into Chad's memories via my mate. How much more fucked up could things get?

But she got me… and I didn't want her to stop. I didn't want this to stop. Maybe it was the mating, or maybe it was that I liked having her total attention. "I wish I was her. She didn't have a selfish bone in her body. She loved my dad every second of her life, even when he was an asshole."

"Well, your father was her child. That's how it works most of the time. As far as I can tell from other people's memories. You love them and you forgive them. Time and again. Your father should be loving you the same way."

Whatever. We were in the rain. And what did it matter? There was a Werewolf coming for my sister-in-law. Why was I here talking to Deacon? Why had I run straight here? Why did Brynna follow me? I…

I'd always supposed I'd know if I was about to have a freak out. I'd have warning. I could take myself some place and do it in private where no one would see. That wasn't how it worked. One second I was okay, and the next, I just wasn't.

I turned my head to the sky and screamed. I fell to my knees. I couldn't even have explained why if asked. My hands tingled. My legs had gone numb. Deacon was there. He said something to me. Brynna was by my side. They were talking. She wiped my wet hair off my face, pressed her head against my shoulder. The smell of roses in the rain. I couldn't stop… fuck, what was I doing? Crying? No. Lyons men didn't cry.

Except I was, and I wasn't stopping. I let my head fall forward. Deacon was still talking but to who? I couldn't hear him over the roar of the rain and thunder. When had the thunder happened? Streaks of light lit up the darkness. Lightning. Lydia was there, a blanket around my shoulders —all of it was vague.

There was so much death. There was nothing. The world my grandmother lived in was long gone. Hundreds of years. Vampires and Werewolves ruled our night. I was so sick of being strong. What did it matter anyway? I fucked up everything, and the woman who made me feel not alone for the first time maybe ever wanted out of this arrangement.

I was brought inside. My shoes came off. I thought I kept telling them all to stop. I thought I twice managed to stop crying. I didn't know. Not for sure.

Because I knew nothing, not really. Just that everything was always hard. Always a small piece of hell, and we never really got to beat back the devil because I fucked everything up and brought them right back.

———

I WIPED AT MY EYES. When had Chad arrived? He sat across from me at Deacon's table. When had I gotten there? Chad silently watched me. "Hey."

He raised his eyebrows. "Hey?"

My whole body hurt like the time I'd had the flu. "Yeah… sorry."

Was there protocol for what to say when you had a nervous breakdown?

"If you say sorry one more time, I'm going to deck you."

Had I said it multiple times? "I don't remember saying it before."

Chad leaned forward. "How long have you been holding on to so much pain?"

Now there was the question of the hour. "What difference does it make?"

"Don't deflect."

Fuck me. I supposed, considering what I'd done, I didn't get to play it cool for at least 24 hours. "I don't even know, Chad."

"Well, none of us are poster children for mental health and nothing we can do about it, anyway. So Jason Kenwood is back. You didn't build the cloning machine. You threw a chair. That's what Brynna said. She went back to see if she could waylay Jason. If he comes back, then we'll deal with him. He's not the end of the world. Rachel picked me. She had herself wiped from people's minds for me. At the end of the day, at this point, he's another Werewolf."

Somehow, I sincerely doubted my brother felt as blasé as he sounded. But, fine. If he wanted to play it this way, we'd do that. "I did this."

"You didn't do anything, but get mated to a Vampire. How's your mating going, by the way?"

I shrugged. "She doesn't want me. She wants out of the mating. Apparently, I'm a manwhore."

"That's what she said? That you're a manwhore?"

"In not so many words." What was complicated about this?

"Huh."

I bent my head. Since we were sharing, I might as well be honest. "I don't understand it when you make noises like that. That sound, that huh or whatever. I don't know what you are thinking or what you want. I'm not smart."

Chad leaned forward and pounded on Deacon's small table. The two water glasses sitting on it somehow leapt in the air and fell back down without spilling. "You're smarter than I am. You always were. You never put your head down and studied. You never took two seconds to give two shits about our classes. You still made decent grades. I had to work all the time. If I'd spent as little time as you, I'd have failed."

"The difference, Chad, is you're physically incapable of failure, and I'm pretty much fine with it."

He patted his chest. "I died, Micah. I'd say that was pretty much failing. Wouldn't you? The me in front of you has different skin than the one I was born with. I'm a copy. That's a pretty big failure."

I hated talking about this. "Look…"

"No." He pointed his finger at me. "You *look*. You freaked out tonight, and I think it was a long time coming. You picked the right person to go to in order to have your eruption. Deacon would step in front of traffic for you if there was such a thing anymore. So would I. Rachel, too, for that matter. And the woman you think believes you to be a manwhore went back underground because she wants to fix this for you. What do you want, Micah? Do you want to disappear underground? Never come back? You could have done so a dozen times now. Do you want to stay here and fight? Not fight? What do *you* want?"

The problem was the answer to his questions changed every day. Every hour. Every minute. "I don't want to stay here and be a lesser version of you to Dad and every person, other than the ones you mentioned, every second of the day. I want to help the effort. And I can't have all of those things all at once. Right now, I also want to destroy every cloning machine ever made and that makes me feel like shit because that's why you're sitting here."

Chad ran his hand over his face. "Then let's do it. Let's be hypocrites. All right, I'm here because of the tech. Well, screw it. I'm tired of these scientists getting to mess with our lives. Let's get rid of their technology. Let's make them live like the rest of us."

I loved the idea of doing something tangible. "Goodbye Dr. Icahn permanently? Goodbye whoever this Doubleday is?"

He pointed at me. "There you are. There's the Micah spark you've been missing for months and months. Looks like you needed this freak out."

"I…" I hated to even think about what had happened. "I can't remember the last few hours. Is that normal?"

Chad shrugged. "Do I seem like a psychiatrist to you? I have no idea what's normal. Our brains have been worked over, or in my case regrown, so many times I can't even begin to imagine how they function at all. Probably not. But which of us are normal anymore?"

An ache passed through my body. "Feel that?"

Chad yawned. "Sure. I guess it's time to go kill Vampires. Can you?"

"Look, I know I lost my mind, but I'm not totally incapable. I'm sure I can take out some Vampires." I got to my feet. I was looser than I'd been in a long time.

"No." Chad laughed. He hadn't stood. "I mean because you're in love with a Vampire. Or former Vampire. So bizarre, but then I'm a clone. So who am I to judge?"

I followed his thinking, finally. "You were there underground. I don't think Brynna has a problem with Vampire killing."

"She didn't watch us do it. So she may not have a problem in theory, but reality? It might be something you need to figure out."

He made a fair point. "I didn't say I was in love with her."

Chad finally got up. "You don't have to. What could

cause a man to lose his shit like that? Love, my brother. Love. Trust me. I spent nights pacing the floors about Rachel. She was with a Werewolf."

I'd have to think about it. After I killed some Vampires. "Are you fighting tonight?"

"Is that what we're calling it these days? Fighting? Keith used to call it patrolling."

Yes, he did. But to me, it had always been fighting, and maybe that's what I missed when it came down to it. I spent too much time in my own head and not enough kicking some ass.

⊏══⊐

WHEN THE SUN ROSE, all the Vampires who had come at us were dead and we weren't. I bent over, holding on to my knees. Deacon stretched his arms toward the sun and nodded toward one of our new Warriors. I didn't know what was more dangerous—a newbie Warrior or an older one who got sloppy?

Right then, I didn't care much. I missed Brynna. This mating thing was going to be a problem. I hadn't thought about her during the fight, but now every cell in my body craved the sight of her like I normally would air or food.

Was she missing me at all?

And just like that, she was there. The sun had come out. Dark circles marred the skin under her eyes. I reached to touch the side of her face and then stopped. I had blood on me. My own, I was afraid. I'd gotten nicked on my own stake. Vampires didn't bleed. They turned to ash.

I didn't want to get blood on her face.

She touched the side of mine instead. "You could die doing this. You know that, right? Sometimes the Vampires win. I mean, no one wins. This isn't what they want to be doing either. But, sometimes they get Warriors."

With her hand on my cheek, the softness of her skin touching my own, I could breathe again. "They haven't gotten me yet."

"Doesn't mean they won't."

She was right. "Look, this is who I am. I can't be docile, all the weeping and losing my mind to the contrary."

Brynna was so quiet. Anxiety prickled at my skin while I waited for her to respond. "You do look better. Getting Chad was the right thing to do. Deacon told me to wait, but he was wrong."

So Brynna had brought Chad to me. "Thank you."

"You're welcome." She dropped her hand but only to lace our fingers together. "What you're saying is if this mating isn't going to drive us both crazy, I need to accept you will risk your life nightly?"

I smirked at her. "I thought you didn't want this. Ending the mating, right?"

"I want this."

Her words banged into my soul like an explosion, but Chad's words of caution from earlier had to be addressed. "I kill Vampires."

She raised her dark, beautiful eyebrows slowly. "I'm not a Vampire anymore. I'm… something else. I don't know what. I don't want to be alone anymore."

"Careful. You now know I'm a crier. I might start again. You're not alone. You have me." I spoke the words and knew they were true. What had cemented this feeling? I didn't know. Maybe it was mating crap, but this felt good, and why should I want it to stop?

She snorted, and then it changed to a downright laugh. I grinned. "Having me is funny?"

"You as a crier is funny. You didn't really cry. You kind of roared. Like a lion. Oh, like your last name. L-Y-O-N. Get it?"

She was clearly not a punner. But she was so adorable I didn't want her to stop. "Totally get it."

"I... I think we need to speak to Margot. About the mating, yes, but I also think she's lying. Shouldn't she have known about Doubleday? Why didn't she say anything?"

Had our doctor been a spy this whole time? The ramifications were concerning. She wouldn't be the first person to betray us if nefarious intent proved to be the case. "Yes. But if we do this, you have to stay. No more running off. You have to live here with me."

"Micah." She looked down at the ground. "Do you think I'd be welcome?"

"Anyone who makes you feel elsewise can answer to me."

And that was all I was going to say on that subject.

———

MARGOT MUST HAVE KNOWN we were coming. She stood, staring out a window with her back stiff, and didn't turn when we entered. She started speaking. "Every cloning machine has a purpose. Icahn kept DNA from everyone who lived here at Genesis on his. That let him decide who he could and couldn't clone. Chad was strategic to have."

She turned. Her eyes were red rimmed. Had she been crying? I didn't interrupt her. When someone wanted to confess their sins, it was best to let them do it without talking them out of the need. Particularly since I needed her intel.

"When he and Rachel were taken prisoner and then

escaped, the time the Vampires killed Chad, I was there. You were too, Brynna. Do you remember?"

My blood turned to ice. Realization dawned on me. Brynna had said she'd turned Warriors into Vampires. "Did you kill my brother?"

"No, but I could have." She looked away from me. "Want to take back the things you said outside? I killed other people's versions of Chad. Lots of brothers, sisters, lovers. The bloodlust hit, and I ended them."

I stared at Margot, ignoring Brynna's question for the moment. "You're pretty manipulative, aren't you? Brynna and I have a falling out now, and you don't have to tell me what I need to know."

She slapped her hand on her forehead. "I'm not trying to be. Sometimes it's hard not to be. I was raised on conspiracy. What do you need to know, Micah?"

"Doubleday. The cloning machines. Where is Icahn? How much have you told all of them?"

Margot visibly shuddered. "Doubleday is like the devil. I only met her once."

"Her?" I'd heard what Margot said, but I'd not processed it before. "Doubleday is a woman?"

The doctor put her hands on her hips. "Women can be the villain, Micah."

"We can deal with Micah's inherent sexism another time. I don't think he'd argue that women can save the day. He's followed Rachel Clancy through Vampire hideouts and practically into the pits of hell. He listens to me. I think it's more like he's shocked women could be bad rather than capable. When I want you to comment on who he is, I'll ask you for it, Margot."

Brynna's fast response startled me. Only Chad ever jumped to my side like that. "I guess I did hear earlier when the scientists said her. I didn't focus. I've had some things on my mind. Back to what we were discussing…"

"Doubleday is scary as fuck. She makes Icahn look tame. My parents, my aunts and uncles, they're terrified of her. Every cloning machine has its purpose. The one where the scientists are cloned is deep in the center of Doubleday's personal lair. You'll find Icahn there. I haven't told them anything. I manipulate to survive, but I don't betray. Brynna should know that." She looked away. Hurt flashing on her features before she turned.

Margot had saved Brynna. Mistrust must hurt. Unless the whole thing was a manipulation.

She spoke again. "I'm not the one you shouldn't trust."

Now that was an interesting statement. Brynna spoke before I could. "Who should we not trust?"

I liked the *we*. "Well, I think his father is probably right up there."

"My dad is many things. An asshole, for sure. But not trustworthy when it comes to Genesis is unlikely."

Margot's eyebrows shot so high I thought they might fly right off her face. "I'm shocked to hear you say that. He practically handed Rachel to Jason's dad to save Genesis, his son's fiancée at the time. That was a big to-do in the studying the Warrior department with Doubleday and, if rumors are true, he told you to sleep with Brynna to get her to do what he wanted."

I looked down at the floor. "I declined. I said no. When I slept with Brynna, it was for myself, not for him."

Cowardice would have me keep my eyes glued to the floor. But I had to see how angry Brynna was going to be. Instead, her face was passive. "I think your point has been made, Margot. He'll do anything for Genesis. Trust him to not be an ass? No. To do what is right for Genesis? Yes. I can see your heart, Micah. Very clearly. Don't worry about

Margot. She means well. She saved my life. A couple of times. She's why I'm free. I'm giving her a few more free passes before I yell at her."

Margot's cheeks reddened. "Come with me."

We walked out of the medical tent, past agriculture to the prison section. We didn't have many people locked up in Genesis, but occasionally, someone did break the law. This was all non-Warrior business. We took care of ourselves most of the time. Policed our own behavior. I didn't know if that was a good thing or a bad thing.

Margot pulled a key out of her pocket and unlocked a padlock on a tent. She removed the device and then unzipped the tent. Were we going into one of the jails? I followed her in, keeping Brynna behind me.

Then I abruptly stopped. I expected prisoners. I got Vampires. Locked up undead, hissing and walking in circles. Brynna gasped. I couldn't believe what I saw, but what got me even more was I couldn't believe what I didn't feel.

"I'm not getting signaled."

Margot pointed toward the locked up Vampires. "No, of course you're not. Just the same way you're not getting them from Brynna. What you react to when you are in the vicinity of Vampires is the smell of their disease. It's like if someone had smoke on them. I was never alive before, but that was how my father used to describe it. Whether he knew he was around a smoker or not, he could smell the old scent of cigarettes they'd inhaled hours earlier. That's what you feel. It's the same kind of reaction. Your bodies were fixed to be physically allergic to the presence of Vampires and Werewolves."

I supposed what she said was interesting, but it didn't answer my question. "Why am I not reacting to those?"

"The scientists decided since Genesis turned on Icahn,

we shouldn't get the benefit of knowing the Vampires were coming anymore. Actually, it was my Uncle Denny. He did it. They're changing the Vamps. Experimenting on them. I told your father. He went with another Warrior and captured five of them. Knows all about this. And hasn't told any of you that you are about to lose your one advantage over the monsters—that you know they're coming. He wants me to experiment on them, see if I can change them back. But my days of experimenting on Vampires are over."

Brynna stepped toward the cages. "I can't see their memories. It's like they're blocked. If I can't see them, they're trapped. They're all alone. The one thing that makes it bearable is the sense of not being alone."

"You really can't be trusted with a secret, can you, Margot?"

My father really needed to wear a bell. We couldn't feel these Vampires or know that my dad was coming, apparently.

"I'm sick of secrets," Margot answered. Unlike earlier, she didn't look ashamed.

I ignored their exchange. What I needed to know before this went any further was how far down this rabbit hole did this whole mess go?

"Dad."

He nodded. "Micah."

Chapter 10

The room wasn't silent. The caged Vampires, made too much racket. I couldn't believe we'd not heard them outside. But, then again, that might just be something else my father was hiding from anyone—soundproof tents.

"You're not going to be easy about this." My father stated the obvious.

I pointed at the Vampires. "You have Vampires locked up in a cage in a non-Warrior area. No one knows they're here. We can't feel them. And none of these things were, I don't know, important enough to tell the Warriors?"

His eyes flared. When I was a kid, I used to fear my father's temper spiking. He didn't frighten me anymore, not in the same way. If it came down to it, I was an inch taller than he was and he was sporting a black eye I'd given him.

"I think it's important. The only advantage we have over them is about to come to an end."

I waited for him to continue, and when he didn't, I had to speak again. "Then why are you hiding this?"

He didn't try to look away. "Why would I tell them?

Why should they worry about what they can't control? And why are you suddenly so interested in the Warriors? You do nothing but try to get away from them."

That was so unfair. Brynna stepped in front of me. "Don't talk to him like that. Why are you like this? Have you been taking care of Genesis for so long you're not even aware when you've crossed a line? You want Margot to experiment on those lost souls? You keep them locked up? You don't tell your own people what they need to know?"

My father ignored her. "Micah, I will keep us all safe by any means necessary. And some day when you're older, you'll understand."

I raised my eyebrows. "I'm twenty-two. I'm not sure your standard age line works at all anymore."

"Your mating has screwed with your head. I can't even believe I had to say that. Mating. Vampires. Former Vampires. Leave it to you to send everything to hell. I don't have to explain this to you, Micah. You'll never be in charge, this won't ever be anything you have to worry about. In the meantime, I can't have you fucking this up."

My father had cursed. I was stuck on such a small point, which was why I didn't feel whatever slammed into the back of my head hit me. The world went black fast.

———

I WOKE up alone in a jail cell, fortunately not surrounded by hungry Vampires. My ears rang, and the world seemed tilted off kilter. I was concussed. Fuck. Again. I didn't know how many times my former Vampire mate or whatever she was now could fix my blasted head.

"Brynna?" I looked around, but only the sound of my own voice filled the jail tent. No one else was with me. Fuck. Fuck. *Fuck*.

I got on my knees and sort of crawled slash stumbled toward the bars. When we'd decided to build this jail, I'd never imagined myself in it. They'd knocked me out and then what? My surge of need for Brynna rocked through me, and I bent my head, waiting for it to stop. How did the Werewolves survive this? If I could manage to live through the night, I was going to figure out how never to be separated from her again.

Maybe I would tie a rope from her wrist to mine. I rubbed my arms. This was getting ridiculous, but what did it even matter? If I was permanently co-dependent, then so be it. I wanted Brynna, and I needed to be the fuck out of here.

"Micah?" I didn't expect to hear my sister's voice through the tent window, but it was Tia for sure.

I touched the side of the tent. "I'm here. What are you doing here?"

"Well, the world is erupting out there, and I got sent to get you out since everyone discounts me anyway."

My pregnant sister must have been messing with the lock since the side of the tent bent slightly. Then she finally poked her head inside to look at me. I supposed we all looked alike, all the Lyons kids. We mostly took after our father's side of the family.

Our mother was lighter than we were in coloring, almost blonde. We were all darker than she was. Tia stepped inside. "Hi."

My little sister had been a terrible Warrior. She'd purposefully gotten herself pregnant at sixteen to avoid having to fight. Her life choices notwithstanding, my nephew was adorable at four years old. She and Glen seemed happy together, and she was having another baby.

Tia could be moody, narcissistic, pushy, and manipulative. She could also be kindhearted and intuitive. I'd never been so happy to see anyone in my life.

"Hello, yourself." I clutched the bars. "I'm dizzy. Did you say the world was exploding?"

"Dad had this idea he could knock you out, imprison you, and somehow subdue your... ah... whatever she is. Girlfriend?"

I pressed my head against the bars. "Can we do labels later? Thank you for coming. Get me out of here or keep talking about important things or whatever."

She rolled her eyes. "You're rambling. You must be really hurt. Your—whatever she is—got away from Dad and had the sense to get to Deacon. He was pissed. Things have exploded. We're getting out of here."

I managed to get to my feet by holding on to the bars. "Brynna's okay?"

"She's fine, I think. I haven't seen her myself. You know, because I'm not a fighting Warrior so no one tells me anything." She pulled a key out of her pocket. I wasn't going to ask her where she got it. Tia opened the lock on my cell. "Lean on me. I won't drop you."

The tiniest bump showed on my sister's lean frame. "Can you manage?"

"I'm pregnant, not dying. I can help you."

Today, assuming it was still the same day, I had been accused of being sexist and now anti-pregnant woman. I was totally pro-woman. They could do whatever they wanted however they wanted to do it. When had everyone started to be so offended by everything I said? Even the things I didn't mean to say. Shit. My head. It pounded.

I leaned on my little sister. I'd never imagined this day would come. Tia was always so... needy. "Where is your child?"

"With Mom. We're headed over there."

Her answer didn't make sense. "Hold on. I thought we were on the Deacon side of Deacon versus Dad. How can we be going to Mom?"

Tia groaned loudly then threw her head back and laughed. Somewhere in the darkness, something exploded. Goosebumps broke out on my skin. I wanted to find Brynna, right then and there. But I was weak—again— and I needed help.

"What is funny?" I rarely understood my sister, ever.

"Our parents aren't together anymore."

I stopped abruptly, nearly falling over. "What?"

"Oh for the love of... Micah, when was the last time you saw them together? It's not like people can get divorced around here. It's not like even if they could, our parents would. They're all kinds of traditional. But, seriously, Dad doesn't even sleep at home anymore. They speak once a day in the square where she tells him about our little brothers, and then... they go about their lives. We're going to Mom's to get you fixed up, get my kid, and get out of here. Before everything explodes."

My parents were divorced? Their marriage had made it through being suspended in time. What in the hell was going on in the world?

And how bad was it I hadn't known? "Does Chad know?"

"Probably not. You all have your heads so far up your asses you never stop to consider life goes on outside of your own little existence. Most people aren't Warriors. Our mother stopped mattering to you and Chad the day you went Upward to fight."

That wasn't true.

Was it?

TIA DEPOSITED me in a chair at my mom's kitchen table. I didn't object. Worry made me want to get up and move, but what was I going to do except get in the way or get myself killed? "Does Brynna know I'm here?"

"I don't know. Glen handed me a key, told me what was happening, and told me to get you. That's as far as my information goes."

"Micah?" My mother stepped out of the back, the gray sweater cardigan she always wore when she was worried draped over her shoulders. She'd had that on when we were put in a cryogenic sleep, and she still had it. I didn't know if anyone else had managed to cross time with their own clothes. Her hair had gotten gray in places, and there were lines near her eyes.

I sat up. "Looks like I got myself beat up again, Mom."

She was at my side, quickly. "Your dad knocked you out. I can hardly believe it."

"If it means anything, I'm pretty sure it was someone else who did the actual knocking. I'm the idiot who didn't realize Dad wasn't alone."

My mother scrunched up her nose. "We're going to get you as fixed up as I can get you and then get you out of here. Genesis is erupting. Again. Believe you me, I'll be having a serious talk with your father."

I grabbed her arm. "Mom, Tia told me something I guess I should have already known."

She looked away from me. "Micah, if there were things I wanted you to know, I'd have found a way to tell you. I can assure you of that. You and Chad, you risk your lives every day. You don't need added burdens. Not telling the two of you was something your father and I agreed on at least. Nothing has changed, not really. We've really not been what I would call happy since we woke up in Genesis.

Oh, who am I kidding? We were not that happy in Before Time either."

My nephew made a squeal in the other room, and we both turned toward the noise. Tia came out, holding him on her hip. He was probably too big for her to carry anymore, but I wasn't going to risk the wrath of Tia by saying anything.

The door to the tent opened, and Chad came in. "Hey, time to go."

"He's not ready. He has a serious head injury," my mother chided.

My brother shrugged. "Nothing much in there to injure, I don't think."

I picked up the salt shaker from the table—someone must have made my mother this in school, and I sincerely hoped it wasn't something beloved—and threw it at him. He ducked out of the way and then pointed at me. "See? He's fine. Besides, Brynna is waiting for him."

The last part got me up. "She okay?"

"Yes. I wanted her to come here, but she's scared of Mom."

"What?" my mother and I answered at the same time. Okay, I got it. Brynna didn't like to be around people. She was constantly worried about being judged unworthy or called a monster. I'd done the last part and might never get over wishing I hadn't.

Tia marched toward Chad. "Wherever we're going, there had better be hot water and heat. My days of following you asses into the middle of nowhere while we come up with a plan are long over."

I held my hand out to my mom. "Grab the boys. Come."

"Oh, Micah." She kissed my cheek. I had to do better by my mom. I had to remember to be there for her more.

Micah

"I'm not coming. I'm going to stay here, deal with your father, and see if I can help calm things down. That's my best use right now. So you can all come home."

If she wasn't leaving, then neither was I. "Then I'll stay."

"No, he has it out for you right now. Thinks he has to separate you from your Vampire girl. He's been manic about it for the last twenty-four hours. If he gets his hands on you, you're going back to jail. Get out of here, Micah. I wish I had time to fix you up."

Tia threw her free hand in the air. "I did the best I could. I had to hide between tents. I couldn't march in there. It's always my fault, right?"

I didn't respond. Instead, I pulled my mom toward me. "If your way doesn't work, come and find us."

"I will. I didn't do a lot right in this world, Micah, or the time before this one. But you were something I must have done well. Look at you."

Chad kicked me in the calf. "Beat up? In the midst of a relationship he can't figure out? Running away in the middle of the night?"

She sighed before she grinned at him. "Strong. Capable. Resilient. Bright. Funny."

"Mom," Tia whined. "You sound like you're writing him a dating ad."

She put out her arms. "I'll tell the little ones you said goodbye." My younger two brothers were adolescents. I highly doubted they liked being referred to as the little ones anymore, but I wasn't going to argue right then. "I sent them to a friend's. I don't want them involved in this yet." My mother wrapped all three of us and her grandson into a hug. She was a tiny woman. I didn't know exactly how she managed, but her arms had always been big enough for all of us. "Be safe wherever you are going, and come

121

back when things have cooled down. He's your father. He really does think he's doing right by everyone, all the time."

They weren't together, and she still had his back. My family dynamics were really fucked up.

———

CHAD HALF DRAGGED ME, but we did eventually get ourselves away from Genesis. I didn't ask him what had been exploding. It hurt too much to talk. It never ceased to amaze me how we were always stumbling onto new places in walking distance from where we lived. That was the problem with being under constant attack. We were always defending ourselves, not moving on.

The building Chad led us to must have been storage at some point. It wasn't falling apart and ancient. Someone had kept it updated. It was a big open space with several rooms to the side, all attached. Maybe it had been a factory?

Inside was Brynna, who grabbed on to me when I came in and buried her face in my arm. I immediately felt better. My head still hurt, but my mind was clearer. How many times was this poor woman going to have to fix me?

"I was terrified. I had no idea where they dragged you. I had to run off."

I couldn't properly tell her all the things I had to say, considering the crowd coming toward us. Instead, I kissed the top of her head. "My family has a unique way of showing each other affection. Sometimes we knock each other out."

"Very funny, Micah."

In the room, joining my mate, Tia, Chad, my nephew, and I were Rachel, Deacon, Lydia, Glen, Ben, Zoe, Martin, and at least three dozen others. It looked like every twenty-something-aged Warrior had come along for the ride.

"You're all out of your minds. Why leave with me?"

Rachel leaned against Chad. "Things are getting more screwed up there by the day. He appoints Deacon, but won't let him lead, not really. Tiffani doesn't have a clue what's going on anymore. He's become an army unto himself. He has Margot locked up somewhere, too. We tried to find her and failed."

"You should stay there and fix this. When it comes down to it, this is an issue between my father and me. No one else needs to get involved."

"It's not so simple." It always shocked me when Glen spoke out. He took his son from Tia. "It's a leadership problem. Your father knew there were Vampires we can't feel running around, and he decided against telling any of us. That's not how this is supposed to be. I mean, sneaking around and lying is Rachel Clancy shit. Not the way the rest of us deal."

My sister-in-law made a squeaking sound. "Hey, Glen, not nice." She looked up at Chad. "Say something, defend me."

"If he said something wrong, I would. You and your martyr complex were a problem for a while, babe."

Things between Chad and Rachel were so easy these days.

Brynna had stayed silent, but she spoke at last. "Listen, I'm a newcomer here. Maybe some of you might actually prefer if I left."

She waited a beat, like she expected someone to say they wanted her gone. I would have killed anyone who did, but as it was, no one said anything. Instead, Deacon answered her. "Come on, jump on into this mess with us, Brynna. You and Micah are a thing now. You get to make as many fucked up decisions as the rest of us do if you want. What do you think?"

"I wanted to say there is so much scary stuff going on out there that Genesis imploding is a terrible idea. Period. But as long as we are all here in this storage hall"—a ha, I had been right—"we might as well use it. Doubleday has Icahn. We need to get to her, and the best thing for everyone would be to let your father cool down and not involve his leadership in this, at all."

Chad nodded. "I agree. I think tonight we hole up in here. Let Micah get his bearings. He has a hard head, but it has been abused a lot lately. We'll go in the morning. All of us. I mean, three dozen people is not exactly stealthy. But nothing works when we try to do it that way, anyway. When was the last time a plan we came up with worked?"

"The time we let Rachel think Deacon betrayed her," Glen helped.

I shook my head. "Deacon's plan. It worked. He also saved the people of Geronimo. He makes good plans."

"That's true," Lydia agreed. "He did, and he does. What do you think, Deacon? You seem to be the man with the plan."

I laughed, even though the sound banged around in my brain. "Let's make that his nickname. The man with the plan."

"Oh, I like." Rachel brightened up.

Deacon groaned. "Anyone calls me the man with the plan, and I'll kick their ass. I actually think Brynna's idea is good. We show up in force. We're not good at stealth. Let's go see what there is to see. All of us together."

And just like that, we had a plan. It might have been a bad one. But what did that matter anymore? All plans were bad. It was about having one to get through one day to the next.

⸻

I LAY on a pad on the floor in one of the small rooms next to the main holding facility of our erstwhile hideaway. Brynna entered quietly. She'd gone to check the surroundings with Deacon. I guessed everything was okay, or we'd have heard otherwise. I hated having her out there without me, but I still nursed a concussion since we'd had no time alone.

"I swear I'm not trying to use you as some medical device."

She snorted. "That's funny. I was hoping you were asleep and I could wake you up in a… fun way."

I didn't move. "Okay, I'll close my eyes."

I let my lids lower until I might as well have been asleep. She climbed over me, her mouth meeting mine. Someday, I would have more time to kiss her. That was really what I wanted. To kiss and kiss Brynna.

"Wake up, Micah."

I feigned sleepiness. "Hi there. How was patrol?"

"Sshh." She kissed my chin, and down further, over my neck. My cock stood at attention. Yes, I liked where this was going. I wanted it. So. Damned. Much.

She breathed against me before she bit down. I cried out. Maybe everyone would hear us. I didn't even care. I touched her everywhere I could while she sucked at my neck.

Wow. I was hard. But I wouldn't embarrass myself. My body buzzed, ready for her, and when she finally let go to kiss me, I all but threw her down on the pad under me. She oomphed then laughed. I touched her everywhere, taking off her clothes and my own as I went. I stroked her deep inside until she came around my fingers. It was such a joy to be able to give her pleasure.

I moved until I could push deep into her core. I closed my eyes. Whatever else there was in the world, right then I was home.

Later, I had her in my arms. "Someday I'll get to take care of you."

"Look, if my weirdness can keep you healthy, then I'm glad it comes in handy. Tell me something about you that I don't know."

That was quite a request. "It'll probably end up with you traveling through a memory with me."

"I know. Is it selfish of me? It's the only thing about being a Vampire I miss. I want to travel before I sleep."

I leaned up on my shoulder. "It's not selfish. Okay, I ran away from home once."

"You did? Where did you go?"

I smiled. "The shore."

The waves had been huge, and no one but locals hung out at the Jersey Shore during the winters. It wasn't anything like the television shows had shown it to be. Even in the summer, the Shore was mostly families. I walked the boardwalk. My parents used to bring us there once a summer, and my mom would hold my father's hand so tight and bring it to her mouth to kiss it sometimes.

My dad would laugh.

I used to love the saltwater taffy and the sounds of the waves.

But at fourteen, having gotten off a bus I shouldn't have been on in the first place, to run away, everything had been scary.

The easy, happy days of summer hadn't followed me to the beach in the middle of January. It had been me, alone in the world, and I'd wondered if anyone would even notice I was gone.

The waves were huge. Scary. Loud. The people on the

boardwalk didn't look happy, rather like they'd have preferred to be anywhere else at all. I kept my head down and wondered if I'd made a terrible mistake.

I couldn't take it anymore. If no one wanted me at home, I wouldn't stay there.

Eventually, my mother had shown up. I never would know how she found me. She'd sat next to me where I dangled my feet off the edge of the boardwalk. My coat wasn't warm enough. Not that I'd ever admit to being cold.

"Ready to go?"

I had been.

I'd never run away again.

In the present, Brynna ran her hand down the side of my face. "The amazing thing about memories is they really can show the world differently, depending on who is doing the remembering. Chad thought you had such a happy childhood."

"Maybe I'm a glass half empty kind of a guy."

She kissed my lips, gently. "Right there with you. We're two pessimists. Nothing to be done about it."

Chapter 11

I supposed I should have asked the night before how anyone knew where Doubleday was. But I was concussed. Again. This last time seriously had to be the last time anyone managed to hit me in the head. All of Brynna's magical healing abilities aside, I was bound to have brain damage if this kept up.

When I asked the Doubleday question, Deacon held up a piece of paper. "This was in the pile of scientific mumbo jumbo you brought back from the lab you two investigated. Lydia spent some time going through the map, pointing to where she should be. Probably a two-day walk."

I looked over my shoulder at my sister, who sat with Lydia and Nero. "Are we bringing everyone?"

"The non-fighters will stay back. I don't think they'll argue too much. For some of these guys, it'll be their first real challenge since Geronimo. Can you help me look out for them?"

I shrugged. "Sure. I try to keep an eye out for the newbies."

"I know you do. Ready to go? You're fixed up like

nothing happened to you. How does the healing work exactly?"

There was no way in hell I'd ever tell him. What happened between Brynna and myself, stayed between Brynna and myself. Forever.

———

IT HAD BEEN a long time since I'd taken a good walk through the woods.

We used to do it all the time back when we'd believed Icahn and felt we were fighting for the good of humanity, not understanding we were, in fact, on the wrong side of history. We were like Icahn's trained fighting monkeys. That had all stopped. If we didn't get control of these people and the shit they kept doing, I was going to end up with my mind erased or changed again. I didn't want to not know who I was.

I think I'd prefer to be dead.

And I didn't think that nonchalantly.

Chad had the map, and we all followed him. Rain started, and my nephew's screams, at first blood curdling, eventually calmed. Glen carried him and kept him dry both in Nero's coat and with Glen's own surrounding him.

"Hey," I called out. It had been silent for a long time, and currently, I didn't think we needed to be that way. "Which one of us gets Nero if you both croak?"

Brynna rolled her eyes. Okay, so maybe I was doing my asshole thing again. I was good at it. I could deflect tension better than anyone else I knew.

Glen laughed. "You, Micah. Tia and I think you would be the perfect person to raise our children."

I waited for Tia to object. When she didn't, I turned to stare at her. There was a challenge in her eyes. "What,

Micah? Are you saying you don't want to raise my son and this baby I'm having? Are you suggesting you would rather not raise them?"

Yeah… I had walked into this one. "In the event both you and Glen die, I would be happy to take any offspring you might have produced by then and raise them right by my side until they are old enough to go be Warriors all on their own."

Brynna squeezed my arm. "They could do a lot worse."

I… I wasn't even sure what to say.

Werewolves suddenly surrounded us, and we hadn't felt them at all. Screams sounded out, and I grabbed my machete off my back. Looked like the Vampires weren't the only ones who had their signals messed with. We hadn't known they were coming.

Brynna didn't have any weapons. "Hun," I called out to her. "Get out of here."

She didn't argue. Instead, she grabbed Nero from Glen and shoved him at Tia. Then my mate took Tia and Lydia by the arms and ran away from the group at her top, unwatchable speed. She wouldn't go far, just enough to not be in the midst of the mess and potentially making things worse.

"If I don't live through this, thank your mate for me, would you?" Glen spoke as we all moved into circles, back-to-back. This was how you fought Werewolves, whether you had warning or not.

"All right," Deacon called out to the newbies. "We're not afraid of these fuckers and…"

The Alpha spoke. It was always bizarre to see a Wolf form with a human voice. Only the Alpha could do it. "We are not here to fight you, human."

"Oh no?" I answered. It should probably have been

Chad or Deacon, but I did it anyway. They could give me crap about it later if they wanted to. It had felt like the Werewolf spoke to me. "This doesn't feel like a friendly visit to me."

"You speak loudly even when you think you are quiet. We heard you back in the warehouse. You are heading for Doubleday."

Great. They knew our plans. "And you're her personal guards? Don't they usually have Vampires for the role? And you're their 'grunt work, keep shit in order' people?"

"Micah," Chad said, warning in his voice. I didn't know what he wanted to say.

I wasn't done. "If you're not here to fight, get to the fucking point."

"We want the boy, Jason Kenwood, that was cloned. He was born to lead us. We need the Kenwoods back. You will get him for us."

I would not. "I've got news for you. I have no intention of getting Jason for anyone. This is not a redo of four years ago. I will not be bringing Jason Kenwood, his father, or Isaac Icahn back to the fray. Some things have to stay done."

"You will bring us the boy, and we will give you a map to every scientist left in the world."

Chad put away his machete. Apparently, he believed that these creatures didn't want to fight. My big brother could be trusting. I'd keep my machete right where it belonged, ready to take off their fucking heads.

"How do we know you have such a map? If such a thing existed, why on earth would you be in possession of it?"

The Alpha shifted from his Wolf form into a human one. As Alpha he could change whenever he wanted. Even during full moons. I checked the sky. The moon wasn't full. It was only one quarter displayed. There had been a time when I had been constantly aware of the moon. My trips down below had made me sloppy. I needed to do better than this.

In his human form, the Alpha had red hair and freckles. He was taller than I was but skinnier. Was he from my time or had he been born in this one? It could go either way with the Werewolves.

"We have the map. We took it when we managed to escape from Doubleday's lair after she experimented on us. We thought to use it eventually for our own means. But Jason is more important."

Werewolves and their logic—they never made sense to me. Why did they want Jason so much?

"Why?" I was actually curious.

"Not helpful right now," Deacon hissed at me. "Let Chad do this. We all have our strengths. This is not yours, brother."

I could have argued, except he was right. Okay, I'd keep quiet. For now, anyway.

Chad finally spoke. "So we get Jason Kenwood out for you, and we, what, trust you to give us this map?"

The Alpha stayed still. "It would be my pleasure to let you deal with the scientists. It would be a dream to have them gone. I cannot express this enough. We hate them."

Well, I supposed we had our hatred in common.

Chad nodded. "Deal, I'll bring you Jason. But if you screw with us, I'm going to let our Wolf Killer burn you to death."

I wondered if Deacon liked that nickname any better than the man with the plan. My lips twitched.

What had it cost my brother emotionally to say he'd bring back Jason? I guessed it didn't matter. All deals in this world were deals with the devil.

WE SPENT the night around a fire, not talking. We couldn't sense the Werewolves, and they could hear us. That meant we couldn't plot. I wished I had a pen and paper. I had a lot of questions. Like how were my brother and his wife doing with this whole thing. Rachel stared at the fire.

I couldn't take any more of the silence. Maybe my need for noise spoke badly of me. People were either comfortable with their own private thoughts or they weren't.

I was clearly not.

"Rachel, I have this memory of you from Before Time."

She raised her gaze to meet mine. "That so?"

"Yes. Remember the time Chad drove you home after Tia ditched you for Glen in the ice skating rink?

My sister groaned, loudly. "I didn't ditch her."

"You kind of did, babe." Glen was more and more chatty these days. I liked it.

Lydia looked between the group. "You all knew each other?"

"A lot of us did, in various ways. There were reasons Icahn picked the crew he did," Rachel spoke. "Micah, I remember the ice skating incident, too. You were with a girl. You left Chad to supervise Tia while you did… whatever."

I'd walked into the discomfort of her bringing up some nameless girl. "I don't even remember her name."

Brynna nudged me. "Want me to tell you?"

Shit. She had that memory. "No. I'm good with remembering no other women but you, Hun."

"What's with the Hun? I haven't agreed to this nickname."

I'd wanted noise, and I'd gotten it. Everyone around the circle cracked up.

"Would you prefer sweetie pie?" I winked at her.

"Only if you want to be called baby cakes." She nudged me. "What gets me about this is you people did things growing up like ice skating."

Rachel leaned toward the fire. "What did you do as a teenager?"

"She's a Manhattan girl. I bet it was sophisticated and interesting." I loved this. If we were home in Genesis and not fighting for our lives out in the woods, I would think I'd never been so happy.

Chad and Glen groaned. It was my brother who spoke. "Are you anti-Jersey, Brynna?"

"I'm working on getting over it." Her eyes twinkled. "I'm convinced I would have run into your brother somewhere along the line anyway."

I pointed at her. "She's older than me. By a few years. So she would have had to go cougaring when she was in grad school and I was in the Navy."

"I thought it was Air Force." Chad raised his eyebrows. "Since you were going against Dad's branch of the military you should, at least, know which one you were going to do."

"What gets me," Deacon inserted himself for the first time, "was you two have had this conversation. How and when you would have met in a fictional future that never happened for either of you."

I threw a rock at him, and he ducked. "This from the guy who stayed to save a town because he liked a girl."

Lydia batted her eyes at Deacon. "And thank goodness he did."

We might have been walking into our deaths. We'd made a deal with the Werewolves—which we knew better than to do—but right then, everything felt easy.

"So in this scenario, are you going off to live with Micah in Jersey when you fall in love and are together?" Deacon sat back.

She fake gasped. "Oh no, he's coming with me to New York City."

"Oh, hell no, I am not." I kicked her foot.

Everyone laughed again.

A memory moved through me. Brynna ran through a park. Her breaths came in and out in short bursts. She was pushing her workout another mile past what she would have normally done. In her ears, a song I didn't know flooded her senses. It was something about a boy breaking someone's heart. It pushed her forward. Snow came down on her nose, and she brushed it away.

Brynna was truly happy.

I was rushed back into my own head, and she touched my knee. "Sorry. I can't control it."

"What happened?" Deacon looked between us. "Feel like I missed something."

"Nothing." I rubbed the back of my neck. I knew something without a doubt—in that Before Time, I would not have made this woman happy. She wanted to run through Central Park, and I would have flown away from there as fast as I possibly could.

Silence hit the fire area again. This time, I didn't try to fill it.

━━━

I DIDN'T HAVE any more time to contemplate what would have worked and not worked in that fictional time, as

Deacon called it, where we weren't stuck fighting monsters. The weather moving in on our position proved brutal. We all took to our tents, and since we didn't have enough, we shared. Brynna and I were pushed in with Deacon and Lydia.

I stared up at the top of the tent and hoped it didn't fold under the assault from the weather. Deacon and Lydia breathed deeply, and next to me, Brynna was silent. I didn't know if she was asleep. We hadn't spent enough time together for me to tell her sleeping habits yet. Most of the time, we were passed out, not resting.

She lifted her head up on her elbow. "Micah?" She barely whispered. I turned my head toward her.

"Hey, go to sleep. Long day tomorrow," I whispered back.

"I made you sad. My running memory. Why?"

I kissed her cheek. "Conversation for another time."

She leaned back down and pushed herself against my side. I closed my eyes. Sleep didn't come right away, but I tried anyway. Why did any of this matter? We weren't those people. We never could be again.

I bit the inside of my cheek to keep from sighing. It mattered because when I looked around at my friends, they'd all ended up with people who would have suited them in any time. Hell, Chad and Rachel, Glen and Tia, there was every chance they'd have been together in Before Time anyway. Tia and Glen had already gotten there when Icahn took them. Deacon and Lydia never lived in Before, and yet they fit like they'd met in a college English class.

I was a stupid romantic, and I wasn't going to think about any of this crap anymore, period.

Dawn came fast, and the rain didn't let up. It didn't matter. We had to get to Doubleday and couldn't wait for sunny skies to do so. Tia, Lydia, Nero—they'd all stay here. In the tents. Dry.

I went out into the rain earlier than I had to, my hand joined with Brynna—the doubts from the night before not relevant now. We headed for Chad's tent. I wanted to give Deacon time alone with Lydia. But Chad's tent wasn't any happier.

"Micah, tell your brother I can still fight."

Chad raised his eyebrows slowly. Yeah, I wasn't going to be telling my brother anything when it came to his wife. Not a damned thing.

"Rachel, I think the fact you're even arguing speaks volumes. When do you listen to me? Since when do you need my permission? You don't feel well, you're not feeling strong, and you know it."

She sank back down. "I suppose you're right."

"Tia, Lydia, the baby—they could use protection." Brynna sat down next to Rachel. "Now they have you."

"Thanks for making me feel better. Or trying." Rachel rubbed her eyes. "Just go. Everything you said was right. All of you go so I can sulk in private and hopefully not do something stupid like have myself erased from your memories."

I was glad she could joke about it. Or maybe she wasn't. I never could really tell with Rachel.

———

THE RAIN NEVER CEASED. Maybe that was why Doubleday's lair looked so completely intimidating. We hadn't really discussed what we would do once we got here because of the Werewolf problem.

Did we walk in?

"One of us knocks on the door," Deacon said aloud.

"The others try to find different ways in. I'll go knock. I can distract them for a bit."

"No," Brynna answered him. "That's not what has to happen."

We all looked at her. Brynna was as smart as anyone I knew. Who better to know how to handle this than my former-Vampire mate?

"What did you have in mind?"

She sighed before she bit down on her bottom lip. My mind was suddenly filled with her memories. I expected to see New York again, but this time it was different. No, this time it was more recent experiences.

The first one took place in the rain. Why did so much of what happened with Brynna involve the rain? She stared down at Genesis. She was cold, tired... terrified. She'd gotten away from the scientists. She'd run for us. But then she'd stopped. Why? We were more frightening to her than all the experimentation in the world. What if we rejected her?

From up on the hill, she saw me. I gasped. I'd never seen myself in someone else's thoughts before. She knew who I was. Chad's memories in particular were vividly filled with me, but other Warriors who had been turned sometimes featured me as well. She thought I was more handsome in person.

I winced. Hard to see myself that way, even if others said it all the time. In her memory, I threw my head back and laughed at something Deacon said. I shook my head. This must have been before Deacon and I left, before Deacon met Lydia.

I walked away, looking down at my feet, and she was filled with the sense I was sad. She stepped back. She'd do this on her own and not make life harder for me or anyone else in Genesis, the last human beacon in the world. As lovely as her view was of us, there was nothing else as appealing as Genesis.

The next visions were the times she saved my life. She watched me a lot. I'd been so clueless. But even as I'd not known, she'd become more and more convinced I had to survive in the world. Keeping me okay meant she was doing something worthwhile.

I stumbled back into the here and now. I was dizzy. "Brynna, what did you do?"

"You all have to survive and go back to Genesis. You have to. You have to fix it with your dad. He's become a shell of the man he should be. Time for him to step down. I will get Jason out for you. If I could have figured out how to do this anywhere but here, I would have done it. I should have died hundreds of years ago. These last few days, I've been free again. Thank you, Micah. You'll be separated from me. Go live."

And suddenly, we were surrounded—by Vampires we couldn't feel. Shouts sounded as everyone realized what was happening. "Brynna," I yelled, reaching for her. "Don't do this."

I wasn't even sure yet what I was begging her not to do. I just knew that she had to not do something.

She stepped away from me, and I needed her touch again. She winced, a sign I hoped meant she hated the separation, too. "Hold on, Micah. The pain won't last too much longer. I can't make you sad anymore."

Brynna had completely misunderstood the reason for my feelings the night before. "No."

"The Vampires won't hurt you unless you try to hurt them. They're all conscious right now. They'll take you back to Rachel. Then you'll need to run, you'll need to fight. That's how long you'll get. Goodbye, Micah."

I rushed to follow her, but a Vampire stepped in my

way. I was surrounded. Herded like sheep away from the woman I had fallen for beyond sense and reason. The Vampires were the border collies, taking us where they wanted to go.

No. Fuck this shit. I would not be taken from her. I surged forward and two Vampires hissed. Chad's arms came around me from behind. "Don't do it. You can't win right now. We're deeply outnumbered. I know how you feel. Rachel pulled this for years. You can't get in between a brave woman and her need to save you. The only thing you can do is go back as soon as we get out of this mess and hope she never does it again. Come on. Sooner we go. Sooner we get back."

With thunder sounding in the sky and Vampires doing my girl a favor by taking us away from this mess, I had the most bizarre experience of my life. We'd walked all day, but it took half the time to return, considering we practically ran to keep from being trampled by the Vamps.

As we finally got back to the tent, I turned and ran. Yes, I was abandoning my brother, Deacon, and the others to fight Vampires. But they'd done it a million times. I turned around to see Deacon nodding at me. They got it. I wouldn't make even a minute difference in a fight. But every second I was away from her was a second she could do something stupid.

Or stupider.

Two Vampires ran after me. We'd apparently reached the fighting portion of the evening. I grabbed my stake and struck them down, wincing as I did so. There would no longer be time when I wouldn't think about how one of them could have been my Brynna in another timeline. Two things went differently on some random Tuesday, and I'd have been staking her instead of loving her.

I ran again, tripping over a root and tumbling before

landing on my feet. I might be beat to shit by the time I got to her, but I'd get there, and so help me, I'd strike down anyone—monster or human—who put themselves between Brynna and me.

It was dark, pitch black, by the time I reached the installation. My head spun, and my heart pounded so hard I wondered if I was going to have a heart attack. I put my hands on my knees. Blood dripped down the side of my face. Some twig got me or something. The whole day was a blur.

A figure stood staring at the building. He was a slight distance away, and it took me ten seconds to realize I looked at the figure of Jason Ulysses Kenwood, Werewolf and one time suitor for Rachel's love.

I'd liked him until I hated him.

And he was here now because I'd brought him back to life.

He turned, sniffing the air, and then saw me. We stared at each other, only the quarter filled moon lighting the night.

"Micah."

I held out my hand. "If you get near me, Jason, I'm going to kill you. My girl is in there. Oh, and if you get anywhere near my sister-in-law, I'll kill you then, too. Or Chad will. Things have changed while you were dead."

It was then it occurred to me he might not have known he'd been dead. Chad hadn't known he was cloned.

"Why the fuck am I here?"

"Well, isn't that the existential question of the universe. Why are any of us here? The Werewolves want you. They're probably not far. Go figure it out with them."

He pointed at the door. "Two guards through there. That's lightweight, considering the rest of the place in there. I can't... I don't know if I can do this again."

I pulled off my machete. "If you want me to end you, I'll go ahead."

It was the least I could do, considering he was here thanks to me.

He shook his head. "We'll see each other again."

I supposed we would. It seemed to be how these things went.

Chapter 12

I knocked on the door. Stake in my left pocket, machete on my back, whoever answered could either let me in or die. I was that serious. I didn't think I'd live to regret their deaths. I was past caring about the outcomes of my decisions. My girl was in there. I needed her. Immediately.

The door swung open, and a Vampire stared at me. They were answering doors now? Brynna had told me staking them was a gift. Fine, I'd dish out some. The Vampire didn't even flinch or back away. The bloodlust must not have been riding him.

A second Vampire rushed toward me, fangs displayed. This one wouldn't be so mellow. That was okay. I had enough adrenaline to take out a whole horde of Vampires if need be. I kicked him back and then staked him.

Breathing heavy, I whirled around. Where to go now?

"Hello, Mr. Lyons," a female voice called out to me as though through a speaker. It echoed off the walls. "You beat my expectations. I thought perhaps we would have to wait until tomorrow to be graced with your presence."

What in the hell? Doubleday had me on some kind of

video feed where she could see me. "How about you come say hello? I want what is mine returned to me immediately."

A small laugh echoed. "And what is yours exactly?"

Four doors I hadn't noticed opened simultaneously. The doors had been made to blend into the wall. Four women wearing different colors of the same long, pencil skirted dress came out. I gasped, for a second not believing my eyes.

Not only was each of the women identical in their dress, save for the colors, they had the same face. And it was one I knew, one I'd seen very recently. It was Margot.

"Oh, I see you recognize me. Or a version of me. Yes," the voice echoing through a speaker continued. "You're seeing what you're seeing, Mr. Lyons."

I was having trouble breathing, but I wouldn't—absolutely couldn't—allow myself to have a breakdown right here. I had to keep it together. Okay, there were... multiple clones in the room with me, and they all looked like Margot.

An older version of the women entered the room. She crossed the space until she was right in front of me. Her dress was exactly the same as the younger versions, except it was black. Or, I highly suspected, everything about those four women was a version of her.

"My name is Christa Doubleday." I stared at her outstretched hand. Did she expect me to shake? She finally dropped her hand. "Oh well, fine. Your generation never had any manners anyway. Do you recognize me?"

I swallowed, forced myself to do so several times before I spoke. "Should I?"

"Well, I was quite famous when the world ended. You must not have watched the news."

I shook my head. "I didn't. I was too busy having sex and fun."

I knew I was being rude, but this woman had something—maybe everything—to do with the end of the world. I didn't have to be polite.

She sighed, putting her hand on her hips. "I believe your mother taught you better, Micah Lyons. I've seen video of you. You know how to behave. Anyway…" She flipped her dark hair over her shoulder. It was long and black. Stick straight, the likes of which I'd never seen.

I knew enough about women to understand grooming. I'd bet my left testicle she was running a hot iron over it every day. What kind of life was she living in this mess of a world she had time for that?

Christa kept speaking. "I was in charge of the response to the Vampire virus. I was the one on television telling everyone not to worry. My husband was a senator. Ring any bells?"

"None." And I knew my answer would make her nuts. This was a person who craved fame, even if it was notoriety in the end.

She threw her head back and laughed. "Oh, I love you. Fine. You didn't know me then, but you know me now. Now, you are here because you want Brynna. Don't worry. You won't soon. I'm breaking that mating. Rather brilliant of 72 to add the Werewolf gene. If I'd known, I'd have stopped her immediately. We don't need any more mating nonsense in this world. It causes enough problems, to be sure."

"My being mated to her has nothing to do with anything. Whether or not she is my mate won't change the fact I'm not leaving here without her. And 72 is Margot?" I had to work really hard to make sure I understood everything going on here.

Her eyes lost some of their glimmer, and heated anger struck out at me instead of whatever this jovial pretense she'd been playing with remained in its place. "I'm afraid you can't have her. Ever. She made me a deal. She came and will let me experiment on her. And in turn, I let Jason Kenwood go. A deal is a deal. You know, I never could have imagined this. When I destroyed the world, that we'd still be here today dealing with things as trivial as sex and love."

"Trivial as sex and love? There's nothing more important."

She tapped my shoulder. "I forgot. You're not as smart as Chad. Ho hum. Fine. You can't have Brynna, so you should run along and get over the idea. You'll feel better in an hour or two. Oh, and Margot, as you called her, doesn't know she's a clone. So if you really want to destroy her life, you can go ahead and tell her."

I took a step back. I knew how I needed to proceed. I had to be sure I got this exactly right. There were four of these women, and as a rule, I didn't hurt anyone of the female sex. Still, I'd brought myself into this mess to rescue Brynna, and rescue her I would.

"Grab him before he does something stupid," the older Doubleday called out.

No, not happening. As two of the women reached for me, I grabbed one and flung her into the other one coming at me. I winced. This was going to be a special kind of hell. "Oh for goodness sake, I'll do it."

She lunged for me, nails out toward my face. They weren't normal human nails but looked more like the Vampires. I dodged out of her way and ran for the door where one of her clones had entered. It shut behind me with a locking sound, and suddenly, I remembered what it had been like to be in a fun house back in the day during one of those summers at the Jersey Shore.

There had been mirrors everywhere, I'd looked really strange in the reflection, and my twelve-year-old self had been silently terrified. There were mirrors all over this room. What in the hell was going on here?

Another Christa walked toward me. She was old, like the one in charge in the other room. Her reflection was everywhere, all-encompassing in the space even though there was technically one of her.

"Hello, Mr. Lyons." New Christa. Back to the Mr. Lyons.

She tilted her head to the side. "Are you confused? You just left me in the room. How am I here?"

Exactly how dumb did she think I was? "No, I'm not confused. I get the whole cloning thing. I didn't stop to think there might be multiples of you running around at the same time, but now I'm understanding what's happened. I'm not leaving here without Brynna. If you want to keep playing games and getting in my way of doing what is going to happen here, I can kill you. I'm not above doing that. I'd even be doing the world a favor, and—wait—you could come back anyway."

She threw her head back and laughed. In every version, this woman had a sick sense of humor. If she didn't look exactly like her, I would say Margot didn't remind me of her at all. She was human, or at least she seemed that way. This woman was a monster.

Arguably worse than the Vampires and Werewolves together.

"Do you think there is more than one Chad here? Do you think I've got five of them tied up in the basement?"

I shook my head. "You're sick in the head, lady. And I'm done."

She ran at me, the claws out again, and this time when I dodged, I shoved her backward. I'd never struck a human woman before. I couldn't really label her as *human*. She wasn't normal, and if I let her, she was going to scratch the crap out of me.

The woman hit the wall hard, and didn't get back up. I ran for the next door. This felt like a game, and I didn't want to play it. Still, what choice did I have really?

She had said something about downstairs. That's where I would head. My mind turned with possibilities. There was no way Margot knew where she came from. What was she? A failed experiment? Something gone wrong? Or what this Christa woman wanted to happen? Some kind of test?

And what did it mean Christa had ended up like this and she was essentially Margot? Was our doctor about to try to take over the world? Not that there was any world to take over anymore. But still, was she bound to be psychotic?

Was this a nature versus nurture thing? The world had ended. Why did I still have to wonder about this shit? Chad still seemed the same as before. The cloning hadn't changed him. Damn it, I didn't know. Margot clearly didn't have the memories of her clone's life. Unless she was really good at faking it. Chad did.

Why did this matter right now?

I knew the answer: because I was freaked out to fucking hell.

Okay, this was a maze. I had always been bad at puzzles. Where was Chad when I needed him? Fine. I'd think this through some. This was a game—I needed Brynna—but I wasn't going to play. They couldn't keep pushing me through doors like some lab rat they wanted to watch. At some point, there would be a way they tried to stop me from going, and that would be the way I went.

I stopped with that thought. Why not start now? They kept moving me forward, fine. I'd go back. I turned and returned to the room where I had been. It was empty now.

"Mr. Lyons," Christa, whichever one she was, spoke over the loudspeaker again. I ignored her like I used to disregard whatever the principal in my high school said. I'd never done well with people who liked to hear the sound of their own voice better than anything else in the world.

There had been four doors. One of them would take me where I wanted to go, and if I ran into a hoard of Christas running around, then I'd deal with them. So far, I'd aptly avoided getting scratched. She wasn't great at defending herself from being shoved. I'd keep shoving.

The first two doors got me nowhere but an empty, doorless, windowless room—the same one—and by the time I reached the third, I had the clones back. Sure enough, there was a staircase. I pushed them all aside and went down. That was good. I didn't feel like pushing off clones while I pressed the walls for whatever trapdoor had to be there so Christa Clones One-Two and however many got in and out.

Margot really lucked out not being trapped here.

The stairs were old. They creaked. No one followed me. That was either really good or really bad news. Maybe I had played right into their hands by simply assuming I'd been clever.

The howl at the bottom of the stairs stopped me in my tracks. Maybe they didn't want to encounter whatever made such a horrific noise. It sounded like a deranged Werewolf.

I swallowed. I dealt with fear all of the time. It wasn't new for me. In fact, lately it seemed like a constant companion. I wasn't afraid of Werewolves. But something about that sound? Yeah, it made my instincts scream to run in the other direction.

Fortunately, my need to get to Brynna was stronger. I pushed open the door and nearly reared back from the stench alone. They must have really good ventilation in the other rooms because I hadn't smelled the stink until I'd come through the door.

Something—or maybe lots of things—was dead in here. The howl again. Since I had no idea what I was doing or where I was going in this deranged fun house, I might as well start with whatever that was. I walked toward the howling and then wished I hadn't. In front of me was a line of cages. It looked like an animal shelter where they would keep the dogs before they euthanized them.

I wished I'd never seen the sight, but Tia had gone through an animal activism phase, and I'd been her chaperone. I had come out of that experience an animal rights guy myself. Tia had moved on from it. I hadn't.

There were humans—sort of—in the cages. I stopped to stare at them. Calling them humans, even in my own mind, stretched the definition. These people had been experimented on. Or cloned badly.

I didn't know which one exactly, but I never wanted to see the distortions to the human figure like this again. Two men had been surgically attached. One guy had two heads. A Werewolf was half shifted and stuck. That explained the howling.

Goosebumps broke out on my body, and if I let myself, I would puke. I battled back from the edge. Whatever else these beings were, they were in pain. I wasn't, and they didn't need to watch me get sick.

What they needed was to be out of their misery.

"Can any of you understand me?"

No one answered, most of them staring straight ahead or rocking back and forth.

Could I do this?

I could. I didn't overthink it. I'd open the doors to the cages, and if any of them came out seeming conscious, I'd leave them alone. They wouldn't make it long outside in the world, but I wouldn't mess with them. The others, I would put out of their misery.

As it was, no one exited their cages. I took my machete, and I did it. Maybe someday someone would go into my head again and mess with my memory. They could have this one. The last one I ended was the half-shifted Werewolf. For a second, before my machete made contact with what was left of its neck, recognition and gratitude appeared in its gaze.

When it was done, I put my hands on my knees and tried to breathe through my nose. Why would Christa have done this to begin with? I needed answers. But first, I needed Brynna. All of this was for her.

How many Vampires had been in pain like that when Christa experimented on them, trying to cure them like she and the other scientists had managed to do with Brynna? How badly had Brynna hurt?

There was a room at the end of the hall, and I walked toward it.

"Micah, you have messed with my zoo. I don't like that."

I didn't care. She was watching me, and she could continue to do so. I was walking out of this mad house with my former Vampire, and if Christa wanted to spend the whole time observing me, she could go ahead. If she sent a million of her deranged clones after me, she could go ahead and do so.

She wasn't going to change any of my plans. "Look,

lady," I called out to the empty room, assuming she could hear me, "I think you and all the versions of yourself you've made have been alone too long. I'm not afraid of you. Keep attacking me. I'm stronger than you are. I will burn this place to the ground with myself inside before I let you keep Brynna here. Do you think I'm lying? I used to blow up Vampire lairs. I'm adept at destruction. Always have been."

Christa could let that sink right in.

And choke on it.

I swung open the door to find myself in another lab. It looked exactly the same as the ones underground and the one we used to have in Genesis. These people liked to keep things consistent. That was for sure.

"Micah," a naked man in a ceiling to floor enclosure called out to me. He was old and looked exactly the same as the last time I'd seen him, save for the nakedness. Isaac Icahn, the most evil man I'd known until I discovered it was possible to be worse than he was. He reached toward me, but I didn't move toward him.

Why hadn't I realized I was going to see him in this place? I shook my head. It didn't matter. He was here, naked, and he seemed to be struggling to breathe.

"She took one of my lungs."

He paused between each word. I shuddered, trying not to feel like my own chest was tight. This was a man who had destroyed us. Played with the minds of everyone I cared for and...

No, he hadn't done that. Not this man. He had the memories of the one who did, but he didn't personally destroy anything. He'd been cloned and hurt. That was it. He wasn't any more responsible for the suffering of humanity than Margot was for Christa.

Chad was basically the same cloned as he'd been

before, but he couldn't be found guilty for things he'd not done.

My head hurt. This was heavy stuff, and I wasn't the right person to deal with these issues. I stepped toward him. "If this is some kind of trick, I'm going to rip your esophagus out and feed it to the next Werewolf I see."

Even if I was willing to see past the fact he looked like my worst nightmare, I wasn't a total idiot.

"I'm going to die. End it before she can do this to me again. Or worse."

I nodded. "I can. She can re-clone you, but for you, yes, I can make the pain stop."

He touched the side of his enclosure. "She can't re-clone me if you get rid of all the machines."

How things changed. He begged Rachel once not to destroy the cloning machines. "No way can we find them all. We know where one is, that's it."

He shook his head, gasping for breath. "Micah, one cloning machine can destroy them all."

"Now, now, Isaac. You don't want to be giving away family secrets." Christa's voice again. "I can make it hurt worse."

She couldn't. I'd kill him first. Icahn kept talking between gasps. "In Genesis, there is a machine. Find it. Buried. Destroy it, and they'll all fry…"

He grabbed his throat. He was choking? What happened? I spun around. Christa was laughing. I would love to know what kind of machine he was talking about, but I wasn't going to get that answer now. I kicked down the door to his enclosure and took off his head.

I couldn't give myself time to think about what I had done in the last ten minutes. Killing monsters to defend Genesis was different than this. I ran further into the medical bay, Christa's laughter following me the whole way. But I found who I looked for. Brynna was strapped to a table, an IV in her arm.

I was at her side before I even realized I'd moved. My body pulled to hers like a magnet. "Brynna."

Her eyes fluttered open. "Micah? What are you doing here?"

"What are they giving you?" I'd talk to her about the hows and why later when I wasn't moments from having beheaded Isaac Icahn. I needed to get her out of there. I knew how to remove an IV. Ours were more basic than this one, but field medicine was something Warriors knew how to do. I could rehydrate a fellow Warrior if need be.

I carefully got the needle out of her arm and pressed a nearby bandage down on it until she stopped bleeding.

Brynna finally spoke again. Her eyes were hooded, and she slurred a bit. "They're weakening my immune system to make me a Vampire again."

Oh hell, they were not. I picked her up in my arms. "Time to go."

"You need to be free of me."

I winced. "You need to stop that nonsense right now."

Christa came around the corner, clapping her hands. "I knew you would do it. Like a rat in a maze, you found your cheese, Micah Lyons. I had to see. How strong was the pull? Could you get to her even with all the horror around you? You did. Bravo. I…"

I shoved the medical table at her, throwing her backward. She could reward herself on a job well done when I was far away from here. I hoped I had killed her. I'd certainly swung the table at her hard enough. "All you've done, lady, is awaken a force you'd rather not have seen. We don't like scientists who play with people's lives. I can promise you that you will rue the day we ever found out you existed."

Her eyes opened, and her gaze hardened, her false joviality fleeing. So much for her being dead. "You won't find that machine. You won't even know what to look for."

I almost told her not to underestimate us, but why would I ever tell my enemy not to make a mistake in battle? Instead, I took my love and ran from the building. No one got in my way. I guessed the experiment was over. That was okay. This rat had found his way out of her deranged maze. At least for now.

I had a feeling she had orchestrated everything I'd done in this sick version of the world. She might have been the puppet master, and me, her unaware marionette. Pinocchio had always been my favorite of the fairy tales my mother read Tia. She wouldn't be pulling my strings anymore.

Chapter 13

Brynna shivered and shook. We weren't going to get back to Genesis or even the tents where we left the others if I didn't get her feeling better soon. A run-down shack with half a roof would have to do.

I picked her up, and the fact that she didn't fight me spoke volumes. She wasn't a pick me up and carry me kind of a girl. I laid her down in the shack, and she scrunched up her face. "You were supposed to be going on with your life, free of the albatross that is me."

I shook my head. "Don't make decisions for me, and I won't make them for you. I don't want to be rid of you. I want..." Oh hell, I was in already. I might as well own the extent of my feelings. "I want to make you happy. Every day. Every second of every day and night. I don't know if I'm the right one to do that. In Before Time, you wouldn't have looked at me twice."

I took off my jacket and tried to put her in it, but she squirmed until I gave up. Her eyes had heat in them. "Micah, I don't even know who the girl is from Before

Time. I don't give a shit what she would have liked and wouldn't have. She went and got made a Vampire. Pretty early in the process of all that mess, too. She wasn't strong. She's part of me, but also not. I'm strong."

"You are." I held up the coat. "You don't want it?"

"That's not going to help."

She shivered like she was cold, but the jacket wasn't going to help? "What will?"

"Blood." She looked down. I hated that the need for it made her ashamed.

I tapped her chin, and she looked up at me. "That's between us. Nothing to ever feel awkward or bad about. I like it. I more than like it. You need to feed, you feed from me. That's how this works. The how and why it happened doesn't fucking matter."

She could curse, and so could I.

Brynna sighed. "Micah, I'm not sure I can stop. I could drain you. Kill you. You're perfectly capable of dying, by the way. The stunt in there makes me want to throttle you. You're not a one man wrecking ball."

I'd never been short of confidence. I smiled at her, slowly. "Sure I am. I got you out, didn't I?"

"That was luck."

I shrugged. "That's me, hun. Lucky." I took her hand, drawing her up. "I trust you. And if you overfeed and I die... well, a guy's gotta go sometime. You sucking on my neck as you make me feel... well, everything? Good way to go."

Tears streamed from her eyes. "I never want to hurt you."

"Then don't. Come on. Stop arguing."

She sighed before she leaned forward farther. She didn't latch, didn't bite down on me. No, she kissed me so slowly right on my mouth that I quit breathing, quit thinking. Her voice was no more than a whisper. "Thank you for saving me, Micah. Thank you. Thank you. Thank you."

She'd whispered, so I did, too. It was that kind of moment. "You're mine. Do you understand? Mine. You never need thank me for jack shit."

Brynna wrapped her arms around my neck. Her breath was warm, and she bit down. I closed my eyes. The immediate surge of heat to my cock came, but unlike other times, the need to do anything about it, the sensation passed fast. I was… content.

She needed blood, and I had it to give to her. The world shifted left. I might collapse, but that was okay. It was a heady feeling.

Brynna pulled back. "You okay? Is it too much?"

She sounded breathy, and I grinned at her. "You're so pretty, Brynna."

Her whole face seemed to beam back at me. How was such a thing possible? "I took slightly too much."

"I'm entirely in love with you."

She put her fingers on my lips. "Tell me those words when you're not hard and high."

I pressed my forehead to hers. She smelled so good. "But I like feeling hard and high. I like how I feel this close to you."

Brynna pushed me back onto the floor and rolled next to me. "I'm not taking advantage of you when you're like this. You're not in your right mind. The two of us suddenly going at it is one thing, you being blood drunk is something else."

"Here's a hint." Why didn't she know this? "I always want you. I'll always want you. You're my wife, right? You can feel free to understand my body is yours."

She went still. Had I said something wrong? "I'm not your wife."

"Isn't that what a mate is, really? It's forever. Like having a wife." I yawned. "Trust me, if you weren't here, I'd be touching myself thinking about you. Fuck, probably shouldn't have said that." I closed my eyes. "I'm going to be that weird guy who said that now. The weird guy you're stuck being mated with. Married. Whatever."

Brynna kissed my cheek. "Sometime when we're not in a shack in the woods, I'm going to ask you to show me how you stroke yourself, thinking of me."

She was the coolest. In this fucked up world. My Vampire was the coolest.

━━

MY HEAD POUNDED, hard. I finally had to give up and open my lids even though I never wanted to again. A cool bit of water hit my lips. I sucked it down. It didn't help. I sat back on my elbows. Brynna was beautiful in the sunlight. But my head hurt like a son of a bitch.

"Hi."

She winced. "You look like hell."

"Well, I feel that way." I touched the side of her face. "But I'm seriously glad you're feeling good. I'd feel this way a million times to make you feel better."

Brynna sighed. "We're not doing this again. I mean, I'm never going to need you to do quite what you did again. I could have killed you. I warned you. I…"

I got to my feet. It wasn't pretty, but I managed it. "What are our issues currently? We're kicked out of Genesis. We have to figure out if we want to do something about my father. Doubleday is scary as fuck, and Margot is a clone. Does that about sum it up?"

She put her hands on her hips. "You're distracting me."

"I don't seem to be doing a good job at it." I pointed to my head. "Not a good day to expect me to be kind and gentle, okay? If you'd rather not put up with my bad mood, feel free to run off and find me tomorrow."

She didn't. Instead, she cupped our hands together. "Those do seem like our problems at present. Since we can't, in fact, change the world back to the way it was."

"Then let's get back to Genesis, deal with my father as a problem first, and find the cloning machine that will kill all other cloning machines."

Brynna nodded. "Guess it is finally time for me to face your friends and family there. I like the ones here. They haven't tried to stake me."

"We do different and odd really well around here. My brother came back from the dead. It's one of those things." I took her in my arms. "Besides, they'd have to get through me if they weren't nice to you."

She sighed. "Micah. How is this happening?"

I smoothed my thumb over her lips. "Let's not worry about how. Let's be glad it is."

"Here they are." My brother's voice sounded in the distance, and we both turned to look at him. "Here they are."

I looked at Brynna. "Do you suppose they tried Doubleday's first before they found us here?"

Chad arrived by our side. His cheeks were red, and he panted. "We have been looking for you two since before dawn. I knew you couldn't be dead in that burned out place. You had to do the burning."

"Burned?" Brynna shook her head. "Did it burn down?"

Deacon came up next to him. "Sure did. Well done, Micah."

I couldn't take credit for what I didn't do. "Not me."

"So what happened?"

I didn't know, but I could almost guarantee—*almost*—some version of Doubleday was out there, waiting to strike again. Immediately, I thought of Margot. How deep into this was she?

"We have to talk." I waited until the rest of them joined us. "First off, Jason is out and running free. I saw him. We talked. That's not the worst news."

Chad shrugged. "He's nothing to me anymore. I got the girl."

I loved my brother's ability to be sure of himself. I'd never stop wondering if Brynna might not have preferred someone else. I shook my head. Not now. I could obsess later. "The other bit is more complicated."

"More complicated than cloning?" I noticed Rachel had gone a little pale. All of her exes running around in the woods again had to be bringing back memories of a time when everything had felt like it might explode.

"Afraid so." I looked at Brynna, and she nodded. They had to know about Margot. "He's not the only clone we need to be concerned about."

———

DEACON HAD BEEN quiet for so long I knew he was stewing. That could either mean he'd gone grumpy on all of us and would be of no use now or he was plotting out something which might actually work. I left Brynna for a moment to fall into step with him. Lydia side-eyed me and then slowed to walk next to Brynna. We were going to arrive at Genesis and make some demands. We weren't even hiding it.

Unless that was about to change because Deacon had a better idea.

"Upset?"

A muscle ticked in Deacon's jaw. "I brought her to Genesis. That was because of me."

Margot... he was talking about her. Yes, he'd nearly been tortured to death, she had been locked up, and when we got to them, she'd saved him. At that point, she'd come along to Genesis. "I don't think she's bad. She's cloned. That doesn't inherently mean evil, right? I mean, look at Chad. He's like the definition of good. If we had a dictionary, it would show his picture under the word good."

Deacon's eyebrows went up. "Dictionary?"

"Never mind." Every once in a while, the fact he'd never lived in Before Time became a problem. Icahn had filled his brain during one of his tamperings with a lot of pop culture. Dictionaries were apparently not one of them.

"But what if she isn't?" He sighed. "Have I once again brought pain down on all of our heads?"

I smirked. "Nah, you're an old married man now. This shit is on me. This is my battle. My father. My problem. Margot falls into the same category. He's got her there with him. This falls right into the Lyons shit. Dad made her our doctor. We'll put this one square on my shoulders."

"You put everything on your shoulders." He shook his head. "Just where you had Apollo tattooed on you. Why did you pick him? You chose all of our tats. Why that one for you?"

I blinked. That was the farthest thing I'd expected to talk about today. "I want to live in the sun. That's all I ever wanted."

I looked over my shoulder as Brynna laughed. She'd

lived most of her existence in the darkness. Maybe we could both figure that out, how to live in daytime. Aloud. And the way we wanted to.

———

"TIA." I stared down the hill at Genesis. "Dad isn't going to shove you in jail with his grandbaby in your stomach. Go get him. Tell him we'll all be in the center of the outdoor habitat in half an hour. He can come and talk to me, or we can battle, his Warriors versus ours. You might remind him who is younger and stronger."

My sister groaned. "I'm not going to threaten him. I'm not stronger. You can go ahead and threaten him if you want to, but I'm going to deliver your message and get out of the way. Besides, I'm sure he has calmed down by now."

———

HE HADN'T.

My father steamed with anger, but to the credit of all of my cohorts, none of us flinched. He yelled and screamed, called us traitors, and I stood there and took it. When he was done telling me all the things wrong with me —or at least a long list of them—I decided it was my turn to talk.

"Once upon a time you, were the one of the most honest, trustworthy, upstanding people on the planet. You didn't break laws. You didn't even bend them. You walked a straight line." I sighed. "And then Isaac Icahn came into our lives and, for some reason, decided he wanted to screw with our family."

I kept my voice low. I'd learned that trick from him. It covered anger. He didn't know if I was calm or if I was mad. That gave me power. He, by contrast, had forgotten himself, and now I knew the depth of how pissed off he was.

I kept speaking. "Your time leading is over. You're unfit. Step down before we have to take you down. I don't think you want to know if I can. And it wouldn't just be me. Your entire family would rise up against you. I don't think that's what you want, right? You kept us alive through startlingly miserable circumstances. But people are starting to suffer. There are Vampires able to get the jump on us now, and we were given no warning. Plus, you have a possible traitor in your midst you know nothing about."

His nostrils flared. I expected him to yell, to scream. But he did nothing. Now just the silent sound of the rain pounding on our heads filled the area around us. No one moved, hardly anyone even seemed to breathe. This was a pivotal moment. I knew it. He knew it. Hell, the universe itself seemed to know it.

"Step down from your leadership role. Go into advisory. Give Chad your place on the council." Maybe it would help if I made sure he understood it wasn't me who was going to take the spot. "Get out of the way before you get us all killed."

The rain picked up. We were all going to be drenched, and we'd lured quite the crowd. The civilians were all around us.

"Micah." He visibly swallowed. "I'm not saying you don't have reasonable points. But…"

Behind me, Brynna gasped. "Vampires. They're here. They're everywhere."

I whirled around. I didn't see anything. I didn't have a signal for any of it, but if she said they were here, they were here. "Friendly?"

Her eyes were huge. "No, love, not at all."

"Incoming," I shouted, knowing it would get everyone's attention. The Warriors ran to cover the space, grabbing their weapons from their packs, moving the way we'd been taught. We had to protect the civilians. Even my father acted. Whatever was about to happen with him, we had a job to do first.

Brynna grabbed my arm. "Something is wrong here. This isn't a feeding, they've somehow been manipulated into thinking they need to massacre everyone. This isn't going to end fast or easily. I'll do what I can."

I kissed her, straight on the lips. "Be careful. I'm so not ready to be a widower yet."

She pursed her lips. "I'm not your wife. If you want me to be, then man up and ask me."

"No, you're my mate. More important, right?"

Brynna lightly shoved me. "Don't get killed, asshat. And stop talking me in circles on this matter. You know what I want."

I did. If we lived through this, I might give it to her.

The Vampires came down the hills in droves. I'd never seen so many at once, and I would have told anyone who asked, up until that moment, I'd seen a ton of them coming at me.

My attention was so fixed on the scene—on the way they seemed to glide rather than walk, in their ability to practically float above the earth—that I didn't even realize my father was next to me.

"I tried to figure out once when I first saw my first Vampire."

It seemed a funny thing to say before battle. "Did you figure it out? Must be Before Time. Like we didn't know that's what they were but those riots and the things happening before cold storage."

He smirked. "Cold storage? Like that. Yes, then. We

had one in lock up in a local police station, and I went with my crew to check him out. Who knew that was going to start a thing?"

Conversation stopped. The Vampires charged, and so did we. There was no hand-to-hand with the Vampires, you either staked and ran, burned them up, or they ended you. It felt like I had grown up doing this. That wasn't true. The first sixteen years of my life had been Vampire-less.

And yet...

My body knew how to do this. Worry for Brynna came and went before coming and going again. She knew how to take care of herself. Chad jumped down the hill, rolling to the ground to drop kick a Vampire getting too close to Glen. Rachel swung from a tree branch, kicking two Vamps in their heads, and then jumped down to stake them. I guessed she was feeling well enough to do that. Or adrenaline had kicked in. She was fine, too.

I struck the Vampire in front of me with my stake. It went down into dust. I wore the green hoodie I'd swiped from one of them once right before the dusting. It wasn't at all easy. I might need to give lessons in doing it sometime.

My mind did this when I battled until it went blank. I knew the nothingness would come. The battle-weary exhaustion where there was only staking, only the death, only the endless. Like realizing that about myself brought it on, I lost myself to the dance. The death dance...

I didn't know how long I fought or how many of them I killed. The only one I became aware of after the fact was the one I didn't kill.

I missed him. Or he dodged. I'm not sure. It happened. A lot. Like a million times, maybe. I missed him. He grabbed my father. It was a funny thing to see. I'd never seen a Vampire grab someone before. Not like this one did.

Scratch. Bite. Wound. Kill. Yes. But he grabbed my father. I reached for him and hit the ground.

Why was I on the ground? I was sort of confused. My breath came and went, came and went. I rose as fast as I could, finally registering that the Vampire dragged my father away. I chased after them. Why would they take him? To turn him. I knew the answer. It had been years since they'd needed to change anyone, but this was how they'd do it.

The Vampire was fast. So much more so than I was. This was the nightmare. We didn't want to be Vampires. What had Brynna said to me? Sometimes they got Warriors, sometimes they changed Warriors, she'd gotten a few herself. My father fought. He struggled. Of course he would. He was strong.

I called out. "Dad, hold on. I'm coming." I ran as hard and fast as I could. "Brynna, help me." I needed her. She was faster than I was, stronger.

I ran. And ran. Somehow, I lost them in the woods. A shout. I followed the sound. Fuck, I couldn't breathe. Why was this so hard? I looked down. I was bleeding from my abdomen. When and what had happened? I didn't even know.

I kept running. Another shout. I got to the scene in time to see Brynna picking the Vampire off my father.

"Hey!" Fuck. I didn't know why I shouted.

The Vampire that Brynna tossed got to his feet. Before I checked on Dad, I had to get rid of him. I jumped on his back. A Deacon move usually, but I wasn't going to be picky. I staked him from the back, right into his heart, and he vanished. I hit the ground into his pile of dust, but rebounded onto my feet a second later.

I reached Brynna, staring down at my father, and his unseeing eyes. "I… No." I was ready to perform CPR. I'd get his heart started again. I knew how. I'd known how even before I was a Warrior. Lifeguarding class to meet women. I knew how.

Brynna squatted down, her hand on my arm. "Micah. He's gone. He's already changing, becoming a Vampire. They turned him. Can't come back once it starts. You can't come back."

"Rachel fought it off." She'd been scratched. She didn't turn.

Were those tears coming down Brynna's face? "Just a scratch. Not full on changing. No one survives this. Not even those immune to it."

Of course, Brynna would know. The memories. I shook my head. "I…"

"I'm so sorry, sweetheart." She'd never called me that before. Weird thought. Everything felt slow. My father was gone. Where had he gone? I… I stood up, nearly knocking Brynna over.

"Why did they do this?" I pointed at my father. "Why take him specifically? They targeted him."

She nodded, rising slowly. "There was some sort of compulsion given during the feeding. I put my thoughts into the mix. They're slowly starting to back off. But to hurt specific targets was in there. All of your friends and family, actually. But not you."

Not me? "Why the fuck not?"

Right then, I'd have been okay with it. Kill me. Take me. A thought dawned on me. Why was I so fucking slow? Why was this taking so long? What was happening? "He's becoming a Vampire."

She looked down. "He is one."

"No, he's not. We can cure him."

"Maybe." She shook her head. "Maybe not. I can take

him. I can bring him to the lab. We can wait and see. If that's what you want."

She was right. I hated her words, but they were truth. He likely couldn't be cured. This was it. This was his end. He was... a Vampire. And all of this was my fault.

I couldn't fix it. I could only... I grabbed my stake.

Out of all the eventualities in the world, out of all the things that had and hadn't happened—even with Chad becoming a Vampire—I'd never imagined this one. I couldn't leave him like this. There was a promise Warriors made to one another. We would never, not any of us, become a Vampire.

I took my stake. It was time. It wasn't a choice. It was a necessity and some sort of dramatic irony I should have seen coming a mile away if I wasn't such a fucking idiot. His eyes flew open, and gone was his usual hardened gaze, instead confusion and the ever-present bloodlust in the eyes of the Vampire wearing my father's body. I lifted my stake. I never gave him a chance to know.

Right there on the cold ground, I staked my father. He dusted. Into nothingness. One second, so present in the world I had to challenge his leadership and the next, dead. Dead. Dead. Dead.

I breathed like I'd run a marathon. Oh, right. I was hurt. Or maybe this was...

Brynna's arms came around me from behind, and I shrugged her off. "Don't."

"Micah." She sounded hurt. "Let me..."

I rose. "No."

The icy wind blasted my face, the rain pounding down.

"I can go." Her voice was low. "I can understand how..."

Enough. "I'm in love with you, Brynna. And if you have to somehow make this about you, about you being a

Vampire, then so be it, but I can't make you feel any better because I can't feel a damned thing."

And she was going to have to live with that.

Being Brynna, she didn't run. I expected her to yell. Instead, she hugged me again. Despite my having told her no. I closed my eyes. Her body was warm. I wasn't ever going to be okay again, or at least not the old version of okay I'd been before tonight. However little okay I actually was.

When it came down to it, I did like the hug.

Chapter 14

Margot stitched my stomach, and it should have hurt. I'd declined the numbing cream she wanted to put on me. A little pain would be wonderful after this huge amount of nothing wafting through me right now.

"Micah? You okay?" Brynna raised her eyebrows.

I shrugged. In the room next door, my sister wept loudly. They'd probably sedate her if she wasn't pregnant. Tia had a way of turning every tragedy we went through to her own personal narrative as though she was the only one going through it. I rubbed my eyes. Maybe I could take a page out of her book. I could start ranting. Yelling might do something about this whole numb thing.

Margot raised her eyes to look at me. "You're done. Micah? Are you hearing me?"

"I'm hearing you." I jumped off the table, and she hissed a breath.

"Careful. You don't want to tear them."

I should ask how many people we lost. I should try to find out if the civilians were okay. I should go see my mother. I should check on my little brothers. My big brother, his pregnant wife. I should know how my nephew was.

I cocked my head to the side. "Have you been betraying us this whole time when we trusted you with our most needy people? Our tiny children? And the secrets we tell no one?"

Margot got to her feet from the stool where she'd sat. Next to me, Brynna shifted. Did she intend to stop me from doing something or help me do it? I couldn't really tell. The whole numb thing. I didn't even know if I cared how Margot answered this, one way or another.

Deacon was suddenly next to me, too. I turned to stare at him. "I was getting ready to ask Margot if she knew she's a clone."

Her eyes widened, and she paled.

I pointed at her. I wasn't reading people really well right now. "Does that look like a response someone would have if they knew?"

Deacon grabbed my arm. "Come on. You're done. You're going to sleep or get wasted. Margot, don't go anywhere. I have questions for you. Brynna, could you watch her for a second? Make sure she doesn't try to run. I'll settle down your guy here, and then we can switch spots."

Brynna nodded. "I could take him."

"I'm not a toddler." I shoved out of his hold. "I don't need to be managed."

Margot bent over, her hands on her knees. "Don't let him break those stitches. I don't think I'm mentally in a position right now to keep my hands steady."

"No one thinks you're a toddler." Deacon's voice was calm. "But you've had a shock and…"

I interrupted him. "A shock? I've had a *shock*? I don't have shocks anymore. Maybe once. In a time you never knew, I could expect things to go a certain way. I could *expect* things in general. Not now. Not anymore. Now, I have to anticipate that everything sucks and it's always worse than I could have imagined. My father being dragged off to die in some sort of plot Margot may or may not have had something to do with? Yeah, I should have seen his death coming. I'm not *shocked*. Frankly, I'm numb. I'm bored. And I'm over this whole fucking thing."

Brynna was in front of me in a flash. Her Vampire speed. I'd never get used to it. "I've got him, Deacon. You stay with Margot. Find out if she did this. I know Doubleday did. But how far this goes, I don't know." Brynna took my hand. "Come. Please. With me. If you need to yell and scream, you can, at me, outside."

I didn't want to yell and scream. "Why would I want to?"

Deacon patted me on the arm. "We got this."

"Got what?" What in the hell was everyone talking about?

Brynna tugged me outside. The cold air hit me but didn't clear my head. "Why can't I think?"

"You don't have to think. You only have to come with me, okay?" We were walking toward my tent. Maybe she was tired. I wasn't. I'd never seen so many people standing outside in the middle of the night. They hushed when we passed, their gazes on us. Were they staring at Brynna because she was a Vampire? I'd fucking end them.

A woman ran up to us, and I caught my breath. She was older, and I knew her because she worked in the mess hall. "Micah, we're all here to support you. Your father was a good man. I know it had gone sour these last few years, but we believe in the Lyons. We believe in you."

"Believe in me?" I stumbled, and only Brynna's hand

on me kept me upright. "Don't believe in me. Believe in Chad if you want to. He's worth it… I'm…"

"Okay." My mate tugged me on. "Thank you. He's exhausted. Thank you for your support."

I wasn't exhausted. Still, when we went into the tent, Brynna laid me down on the bed and drew me to her. I let her. She held my head to her chest, and I could hear her heartbeat. Strong. Steady. Amazing that it did. I closed my eyes. "Do you need to feed?"

"Sshh. No. I think you need to feed more than I do, but neither of us is going to worry about hunger right now."

I closed my eyes.

———

THE WIND HOWLED, the snow came down on our heads in heaps, yet we all braved the cold for my father's funeral. The ground was frozen, so we hadn't even dug an empty grave to commemorate him. He'd have an empty urn instead. My mother wanted to come up for the funeral. He'd apparently "spent enough of his life underground," and so here we all were freezing.

What had I learned in the two days since his death? I kept asking myself that, because it was what he once would have asked me.

"What did you learn failing the exam, Micah?"

"What did you learn crashing the car, Micah?"

What had I learned since I got my father killed? Well, there were all kinds of grief. There was a grief of what was not said. The grief of what was. Would I have unmanned my father in front of everyone he knew if I'd known he was going to die? No. Should I have done it in any case? Should I have done it if I'd known he would live fifty years? No.

"You know what," my sister called out, interrupting Tiffani. She'd been saying something about my father's heart for service. I hadn't really been listening.

What have you learned, Micah? Well, I don't much care what anyone says most of the time.

Tia rose. "Dad's on his way here, now. I mean, let's face it, everyone gets cloned, right? Chad's a clone. Margot's a clone." She had been cleared from all wrongdoing. I didn't know if believing her was a good thing or a bad thing. What did it matter? Life sucked. "I bet he's on his way here. Let's not mourn him. Let's be happy he's coming back. Hell, even Jason is out there somewhere."

"Sit. Down. Tia." Chad spoke through clenched teeth.

Glen shook his head. "Don't talk to her like that."

Even in death, there was nothing more divisive than my dad. Here he was, splitting up the family again. And he was only here in metaphor or symbolically or some shit. I laughed. That wasn't appropriate, but I'd long since passed over the line of civility.

What have you learned, Micah? Well, I'm a little bit fucked in the head.

Tiffani called out, "Keith has not been cloned."

All right, I'd had enough. Beside me, Brynna shifted in her seat. My mate was turning out to be seriously there for me all the time. Maybe when I stopped being so screwed up, I could thank her.

I rose. "You people have no idea what you're talking about when you talk about clones." I rocked back on my feet. "You've seen the ones they lose. Chad. Margot." She winced. The doctor really hadn't like being cloned. "Icahn when he was here. But this whole thing can and does go wrong. Or they can make it go wrong. A whole house of them. Three arms. Half a liver. Two heads." The mess of the place, the sheer horror of a funhouse gone so distorted it would never, ever leave my mind. "People screaming for help. My father wouldn't have the slightest idea how to handle this." And here I was, betraying him in memory, speaking ill of the dead. But messing up was what I did. "None. I don't know what to do or if there is even anything to do about it." I looked down at the snow. "Don't listen to me. Don't talk to me. Don't trust me. I know very little. What I do believe is he loved you, Tia. From the moment you were born, you were his girl. And, Luke and Ashton." My younger brothers, they had to know. "I remember when you were born, he was so happy. He loved you. And Chad." I nodded at my oldest brother so he'd understand what I couldn't even say. "You were everything. You were all his legacy. You were everything. Mom, I…"

She rose slowly. "Micah, you didn't know him. Not when I first met him. He was you. Or somewhat like you. You're kinder than he ever was. But don't assume how he ended or the middle bit was how he started out." Her voice broke. "He wasn't perfect, but he loved his family and tried to keep everyone safe."

That seemed to be the last statement on the matter. The funeral broke up afterward, and most of the civilians who had come decided to go back underground. It was funny. We'd all hated the below ground existence, but up against the snow, some of the population chose to go back down until spring. Like bears hibernating…

"He loved you, and at the same time, he knew he wasn't a good father to you."

I stopped. Brynna had been so quiet I hadn't even known she was behind me. I both wanted to reach for her and to tell her to leave me alone. I'd never been such a battle of emotions ever.

I shut my eyes. "You know that how?"

"I have his memories."

Well, that was news to me. I lifted my lids. "What? He was a Vampire for three seconds."

"Nevertheless, they passed to the hive mind, and here I am with them. I've struggled with what to tell you. I have to say, your mother is wrong. You are not your father. You're what he should have been." She touched my arm. "That being said, he did love you."

She sucked in a breath, her eyes distant. Suddenly, a memory moved through me. It took me a moment to recognize myself as a toddler. My face was rounder, my eyes seemingly bigger. I was on my father's shoulders, which meant I saw myself from below. He laughed at something I said. It changed. He threw me a ball, and I caught it, easily. Pride wafted through him. Instance after instance flew through my consciousness until a recent one came into view.

I was coming back from having been gone, under-ground. One of my many trips there and back again. I had a group I'd rescued with me. He was so... proud of me. I almost fell over from the sheer magnitude. I'd had no idea. He seemed so annoyed with me all the time.

Brynna squeezed my hand. "He was, a lot. Annoyed. I mean, I hate to say it, but we can't go around romanticizing the dead, right? Sometimes he was proud. He always loved you. I think he wasn't a good father to you, but I've never been a parent. How am I to know what it's like? Memories aren't the same as living it. I don't even know if I can be fixed to have children. My body doesn't exactly work like other people's. Would the baby be a bloodsucker? Sorry, I'm rambling."

I tugged her into my arms. "You gave me a gift. Not one I expected to have. I've got a sense he loved me. You're right, it doesn't undo everything that happened with us. It doesn't make it okay. I don't know why in a family of five he picked one child to dislike some of the time. I'm not going to try to analyze it too much. My turn to ramble. Knowing he loved me, knowing for sure, it's something. And I don't want kids. I like other people's, but I'd really rather not. We didn't really get to have this conversation before we did this. So, yeah. What do you think?"

She sighed. "Relieved. I don't want to keep anyone alive but myself. And you. Can we do life that way?"

"For sure." I didn't even feel a twinge of disappointment. No babies. Not for us.

I WALKED through the snow at my father's side. We both wore leather jackets, which was what cued me into the fact I was dreaming. I'd never owned a leather coat. Not even in Before Time.

"I did things wrong when it came to Genesis. I didn't see big picture."

I shrugged. "You took us from underground to above again. Kept us all alive. You're dead. I'm not going to criticize."

He smirked at me as we approached the cliff above the Hudson River. No one called it the Hudson River anymore, but that was what it was. I looked down. There was ice floating on the river. It was that cold, but I couldn't feel it. Not with my spiffy leather coat on.

"You sure will and a lot. Some of it will be fair. Some of it will be unfair. That's okay. I'm not here to hear it, so don't obsess."

I stared at his profile. We did look alike. That was for sure. "And you've come back from the dead to teach me to grieve?"

"This is your dream. You tell me why I'm here."

I nodded. He was right. "You're here because you screwed some things up. You didn't think big picture." I used the phrases he had earlier. "I have to remember to do that. I have to find and destroy the cloning machine that will destroy all the others. I have to pay attention to what you didn't. And it has to be me because Chad just took on the role that you had, which made it impossible for you to think like you should have."

The snow picked up, and I started to lose sight of him. He faded in the snow, like a picture losing its resolution.

"I wouldn't have agreed to what you had to do. Chad will."

I sat up in bed, my heart in my throat, my ears ringing. Brynna jumped up. "What's wrong? Bad dream?"

"No, more like a clear head. We have to find the machine. I can't be sleeping. Doubleday sent Vampires to kill my people. She only got one and probably because he was so out of practice fighting he had no business doing it anymore. And yet…" I jumped out of bed. "We need that machine."

She touched my biceps. "Yes, we do. Right now?"

"No time to lose. They're going to come back."

She unzipped the tent and then quickly zipped it closed again. "Not tonight. No one is getting anywhere tonight. We're snowed in."

I sat right back down on the bed. "Of course we are. Fuck. What is the matter with me?"

"Your father died."

I beamed at her as she stood right over me. "Yeah, other than the obvious."

"Were you only thinking about the machine, or was there anything else?"

I leaned back on my elbows. Maybe I could show her. "Do you want to see what I'm thinking?"

She lifted her eyebrows. This woman was so beautiful. "I can't read your mind. You've never been made a Vampire. I don't have your memories. I can share them sometimes, but I can't control when."

I grinned. "There are lots of ways to show people things."

I leaped out of bed and grabbed a pen. There was little to write on, but the back of an instruction manual for one of the agricultural machines would work fine. Why did I even have this thing? I needed to clean this place out.

I started to draw. Circle upon circle. "Here's the thing. Imagine Genesis is the center. We have no support. We're sitting here like, okay, whoever wants to attack us, come and get us. Even Geronimo had better fortification. They at least had a wall."

She kneeled down. "Are you suggesting building a wall?"

"Among other things. This is still Icahn's design here. This is still what he left us with. It's time to be proactive. This isn't their world. It's ours. We have to take it back, and the first bit is to say Genesis is fortified. The Warriors, some of them can continue to patrol inside, but the wall will have a fort." I drew it in. "That's where we stay. That's where we create the first barrier to keep them out. We hold the wall. If it falls, there is another wall. If we find Vampire holds, we plug them. We work on electricity. A beacon in the darkness for any humans out there. Come to us. They have to be vetted, but we'll figure that out."

As I drew, the whole scene showed itself to me. This was what we'd been missing and why it had felt so wrong here to me. "They can only keep getting to us if we let them. Our engineering and construction crews can do this. It'll take some time, but they can."

She nodded. "Micah, who mans the fort?"

"The new Warriors when they're ready to fight. In their second year of training. And we alternate various veteran Warriors in and out. Someone will have to man it full time."

Brynna twisted her lips. "Someone?"

She had read this correctly. "Okay, me. If you're okay with the idea. I don't go anywhere without you."

I wasn't even afraid of us being together anymore.

She stroked the side of my face. "I'm good with this. I think I could even be helpful. I'm strong and tough. I can hear them coming. I like giving it more of a space between the civilians and here. I like being able to know I've helped make a difference. It might feel like redemption."

"Oh, babe." I stroked a finger down the side of her face. "You have nothing to be redeemed for."

"That's a matter of opinion."

Yes, but I was right, and she was wrong. That was something she'd have to get used to.

I'd show it to her over the next twenty years. That was about as long as we got these days. If I made it to forty, I'd be thrilled.

She touched where I'd drawn—badly—my plan for what we had to do now. She raised her gaze to meet mine. "But first the cloning machine."

But first that.

━━━

THE SECOND THE storm let up, I was out of my tent and heading for the below ground part of Genesis. I should have been surprised Rachel and Chad were there too, but I wasn't. They'd have felt the same need to do something.

With Brynna joining us, we took the squeaky elevator down into what had once been both our prison and our home. Unlike the holes in the ground where the Vampires were held, the Genesis shaft had been designed for personal transport. It felt like I was going to plummet to my death half the time, but it hadn't faltered yet. We'd so far lived to tell the tale of our travels up and down.

The elevator opened to Deacon leaning against the back wall. "Figured you guys were coming. Lydia and I started brainstorming some stuff last night about where the cloning machine might be. We're going to have to tear this place up."

"I had some ideas myself but not about where. Things I need to talk to the council about. Big ideas."

Chad raised his eyebrows. "Tell me."

"After we find and destroy this mess." I looked at Rachel. She had a funny look on her face. "What's up?"

She put her hands on her hips. "You know, all this time, I've known something and not known it."

Brynna took my hand in hers. "I know that feeling very well."

"Right after we got married, my father-in-law woke me up. There was a message from Icahn on how to kill all the Vampires, if we wanted to. I couldn't make that kind of decision. It involved poisoning the food supply. The humans. I wouldn't do it. He decided against it, too. It always bothered me. A lot of things about that. The way that info was just waiting there for us on that particular day."

I remembered the day well. "The destroyed lab. It's a junk place now."

"Is it? Or are we missing something altogether? How

did that stuff get in there on exactly that day? Maybe it's not related. Maybe… it's nothing. I don't know. I think it might be worth taking a good look in that room."

Chad nodded. "I vote for yes."

Glen rounded the corner, out of breath. "Damn it, you beat me here. I thought I'd be early."

I laughed. The kind of burst that took me by surprise, and soon I had my hands on my knees as I tried to breathe through my nose to stop. We had all shown up thinking we'd had the idea to go searching before anyone else. I didn't know why all of us being the same was funny. Sometimes things were for no reason at all.

"If Micah is done making a scene"—Chad had amusement in his eyes—"let's go check out the junk lab."

Glen made a sound somewhere between an ooh and ahh. "I love the junk lab."

Deacon slapped him on the back. "I know you do, buddy. If you hadn't shown up, we'd have had to come and get you."

We were the people in charge now. I really hoped we managed not to burn down the world.

Chapter 15

I stood in the lab two floors below our underground lair and sighed. At what point during the last few years had this become a requisite garbage dump? Or at least a place where everyone shoved their old stuff that didn't work anymore? We didn't have that much tech, but all of it that was broken seemed to be right here.

Glen spun in a circle. "What I could do in here. I mean, I could make a lot of this work again or make new things out of them."

I turned to him. "So why don't you?"

He shrugged. "How can I keep up my Warrior duties, raise what is about to be two kids, spend time with Tia, and work on tech? I don't have free time to do it."

"Glen." I couldn't believe I was about to give anyone advice. "Life is short and over in a second. You are an incredible Warrior. I can think of a dozen times you saved my ass. But you're my family, so I'm going to say this to you. Do what you want. We have a lot of Warriors. We're training really well. Everyone isn't dying from being ill prepared anymore. You can step down." I winced. "I'm not council. Chad? Deacon?"

Deacon nodded. "I think it's a great idea. Fix our tech, Glen. That's your job. Help fight if we need it. Train like twice a week, early in the morning, to stay sharp. That'll give you more time with the baby, too."

"You're council." Chad glared at me. "Or you'll be some kind of advisory thing."

I ignored him for now. "Could you make the lights work? I mean, fuck. I need to talk to you guys about this idea I had. I was going to wait. But listen, I think I know how to fix things. Some of them, anyway."

All eyes were on me, and Brynna leaned slightly into me, showing me her support. I opened my mouth, and it all flew out. The way we had to redo Genesis. What it would take. It would be a massive undertaking. I wasn't negating the sheer amount of work, but in two years, if we really devoted ourselves to getting it done, we'd be where we needed to be.

When I finished, they were silent. The weight of having said something stupid ran through me like I was back in school getting all the wrong answers on everything. I knew how to handle this kind of eventuality. I'd done so many times.

I made myself a joke.

"Oh, fuck it, don't listen to me. I'll stick to looking in the mirror. I'm good at grooming."

Chad raised both his eyebrows. "I think it's brilliant. I think that's what we should have been doing since I was nineteen. I mean, yeah. This is great. Perfect. I mean, I'm sure there are things we'll have to tweak."

Rachel grinned. "Like we're saying we are devoted to not living day by day but to an actual future where things are better. We can keep pushing out the exterior. Once we have the section you make under control, we wait five years and we push out again."

"What about Doubleday?" Lydia linked hands with Deacon. "What do we do about her?"

"We let her die." Brynna shot out. "We find this damned cloning machine, we let Glen figure out how to turn it off so she can't make any more, and then we let them all die. At some point, even if it's not our generation, we outlive them. The Vampires lose food supplies if we manage to get most of the human population here, and we use the Warriors that want to be involved to continue Micah's work of emptying the underground tunnels."

I sighed. "You make that sound easy."

"No, not easy, just goals we can reach." Brynna seemed so sure of this plan. I wondered if she meant it or if she was on my side in general. Did it matter? No. I was glad to have her support. Although everyone in this room seemed to think I was on to something here.

This was a first.

"I have one objection." Chad scratched his head.

And here it was. The whole thing would fall apart now. "What?"

"In this plan, someone lives in the fort. Someone is permanently there running things. Taking all the risks."

Where was he going with this? "Someone would have to be. Yes, for this to work. The others—the young Warriors and the established ones rotate in and off. We'd come up with a schedule."

"And you're the permanent Warrior, right? I mean you haven't officially said you are, but that's what we're talking about."

Deacon shifted his feet. "Shit."

"What's the problem?" I raised my voice. My patience was thin. That had to be true for all of us after what had happened with Dad, and yet here we were, pressing on like he'd wanted us to do every time there was tragedy. Dad had even pushed forward when Chad died. That had been hard but…

Fuck, my mind was wandering, again.

"The problem with that," Chad hollered back to me, officially losing his cool, which was weird for him, "is I don't want my brother facing down danger every day for the rest of his life. Okay? I mean that doesn't sound right. We all face danger. But you know the person in that fort is going to live it, day in and day out, all the time. Excuse me if I don't want it to be you."

The fact that Chad was losing it threw me off my angry hill. He'd lost our father, too, and we'd hardly even discussed it. We'd always been close. In Before Time. Now. There had never been a time when Chad and I hadn't had each other's backs.

"I won't be alone." I nodded toward Brynna. "My gorgeous woman says she's down with doing this with me."

Deacon scrunched up his face. "Down."

"Slang," Chad and I said together. We'd never had a ton in common, but every once in a while, it was like we suddenly had everything alike.

"Gotcha." Deacon walked in between us and put a hand on both our arms. "I'll miss him, too, Chad. A lot. But he'll have to come in regularly, and we both know he's the right one for the job. Particularly if his wife is going with him. I watched her fight during that last battle. She's tough."

She'd been fighting. I turned to look at her, and she shrugged. Obviously, we weren't going to talk about it right now. Why was this the first time I'd heard about this?

"Chad, I'm not made for safety. That's not my journey.

I won't take unnecessary risks. You can be certain I'll hold the wall."

Glen cleared his throat. "Sorry to interrupt, but I found it."

"What?"

Deacon let go of my arm. "The cloning machine?"

"Well, it's not exactly a cloning machine. I mean how could there be a cloning machine? They're huge. Giant water tanks. It's a whole thing. Not like we know it. But there's no way we wouldn't have seen that. I mean, I suppose there are other hidden labs but…"

"Glen." Rachel squatted next to him. "You're rambling."

He grimaced. "Sorry. Here." He held up what looked like an old fax machine. What was that even doing here? Who was there to fax? "This isn't what it looks like."

Deacon and Lydia looked at each other and then at Glen. Yep, neither of them would know what it looked like. I'd give him my best explanation for it later. He raised it higher. "They wouldn't have started with cloning people. They'd have to have started with something else. I…" He winced. "I need to study this. If I was a mad genius that wanted to rule the world, I'd store all of the cloning data somewhere. Like a mother system that controls all the others."

A mother system that controlled all the others? What was my sister doing to him? That was a question for another time.

"Why would they keep it here?" Brynna put a hand on the machine. She did that a lot. Brynna liked tactical contact with things. I didn't mind. It meant her hand was constantly on me.

Glen rose, the device in his hand. "Speculation? They wanted to be able to send things here. To clone as they pleased. Remember the killing the Vampires potion? That was here. It showed up with that video right when it did? Maybe they sent it that day. Or, maybe it was some kind of control thing. Icahn held on to it here, away from Double-day, to try to prevent her from doing what she ultimately did."

My brother-in-law, Glen, the man my father always hated.

He might be the savior of us all.

"I think…"

Brynna sucked in a breath, and seconds later, we all felt what had made her gasp. There were Vampires here. They weren't the Vampires we couldn't feel. These were good old-fashioned, signal-giving Vampires. And they were here.

Why? Glen paled. "I wonder if they know I have it."

"Doubleday didn't think we'd find it."

I understood in an instant what had to happen, and I moved as fast as I could. I grabbed on to Glen. Whatever battle took place next, he had to live to take care of that cloning machine. He had to get it shut down.

"Look at me." I kept my voice low as I dragged Glen toward the ladder. "Hide. Take this and hide. Don't take it to my sister. Get out of here before the Vampires get you. Hide. Get it shut down before you come back. We won't let them get to you. In fact, Deacon, Lydia, go with him. He needs protection. Go now."

I wasn't in charge of them; in fact, just the opposite was true. Yet, they all took off like I was the leader of this show. They hauled ass up the ladder before I whirled around. If I could, I would push everyone in this room out.

Brynna. Chad. Rachel. They were my family. But family was the problem. When you were a family of Warriors, death—yours or monsters'—was the end to every day. Doubleday hadn't hurt me enough. I'd won her maze, beaten her challenge, and now she meant to make me pay for it.

If I asked them to leave, they wouldn't.

"Brynna, what's the deal?"

She pursed her lips. "They're lost to the need to feed. She must have been starving them for a long time. I can't insert myself in there. Not yet. They're coming through the wall."

I could hear the scratches, the bangs.

"Rachel, Brynna, go evacuate the civilian population down here. Please." That was a legitimate request. "Get them out. Get the other Warriors activated if Deacon hasn't already."

Chad took a long inhale. "Stay away, Rachel. Keep her safe."

She looked like she might argue and then didn't. "I will."

"Did you find out for sure you're having a girl?" I might never meet my niece or nephew, but I liked knowing they were coming.

"We're not finding out. That's a Before Time luxury. I know it's a girl. I can feel it. Elizabeth. That's her name." He rubbed his forehead. "Although she might not know me, I know her."

My whole body went cold. Elizabeth couldn't not know Chad. Not for this bullshit. Not for this endless amount of crap I'd foisted on us all by not dying in that madhouse Doubleday had been running.

Like I'd known with Glen, I understood immediately what had to happen. For the first time in my life, I fully grasped what it had taken for Rachel to do the things she'd done all those years ago. It had seemed like constant martyrdom, but she'd loved us that much.

"Chad, I'm sorry. That's not at all an acceptable response."

He never expected me to punch him. If he had, he'd certainly not have expected it to be a knockout blow. Brynna gasped, and Rachel groaned as Chad hit the floor. I looked up at his wife. "He has to meet Elizabeth."

"Micah, he's going to kill you." She spoke through gritted teeth. "You can't do this alone."

Brynna spoke softly. "He won't. I'm here. Get the other Warriors."

I hoisted Chad over my shoulder. He was heavy, but I was strong. I climbed the ladder as fast as I could. Rachel followed closely. I laid him down and turned to see a Warrior running over. He was older but a good fighter, and he'd never been too much of a kiss ass to my father. His name was Daniel. I'd never spoken a word to him before, but Daniel was going to help me now.

"Grab my brother, drag him away somewhere safe. Okay?"

Daniel looked down at Chad. "Is he okay?"

"He'll be fine. Take him. Now. Thanks." I didn't give him a chance to ask me any questions. I turned toward Rachel. She was pale. "Rachel, tell him…" I wasn't able to finish. I didn't know what I would say.

"Tell him once *she* had a name it was too much. I get it. He'll never forgive you." She threw her arms around me, and I hugged her tightly. We'd been such close friends for years before she was family. "Don't die, Micah."

I found my words. "You and I both know the chances are slim I'm going to get out of this. But I'll keep them from getting up here. As long as I can."

She pulled back. "You're playing the role I used to play."

"How am I doing?"

Rachel wiped tears from her eyes, and I ignored them. "Really well."

I climbed back down the ladder. Brynna stared at a small hole in the wall. We didn't have time before they made the small hole a big hole. I'd promised to hold them back. As long as the wall was a one-person sized hole, we had a chance. But in the event we didn't, the Vampires could stay down here. Forever.

I grabbed the ladder. "Brynna, help me, love. We need to break apart this ladder."

"Good call." She was stronger than me even though she'd denied that once. Soon, using her hands, she'd torn apart the wooden ladder until it was all over the floor. Her gaze stayed on the ground. "Extra stake materials."

"Brynna, I love you." I had to say it. Needed to say it. Was desperate to shout it from the rooftops until it vibrated off the walls.

She linked our hands. "I love you, too. And I know this is goodbye. So thank you for making me feel human again for the first time in hundreds of years."

"You and I should have been gone long ago. This is captured time." I realized I meant it as I said it. "Thanks for making me feel alive. Thanks for waking me up."

A Vampire-sized hole came through the wall followed immediately by a Vampire. The Warriors gathered above us. They'd catch them if they got up there. Genesis would stand. It had always been everything.

Before Brynna. Now she was everything.

⊏⊐

MY FATHER once said to me, when it came to bullets, you never heard the one that got you. You were shot, but you never heard it hit. It turned out the same thing happened when a Vampire that wasn't your mate got ahold of your neck.

I didn't hear it. Didn't feel it. He took me straight to the ground, his body on top of mine like we were lovers. I was dead. He'd torn into my neck in such a fashion I knew I wasn't coming back. Brynna screamed in the distance, seeing me. Vampires, all of them circling her, surrounded her.

Everything felt distant... blood loss. Shock. Others screamed through this death. Maybe it was a mercy I couldn't feel a thing. He raised his bleeding wrist. Why was the Vampire bleeding? He pressed it to my mouth. No, I knew what that meant. But I had no strength. Just the fog of death to drag me under.

BLOOD. My mouth watered. My ears rang. There was nothing else, only the need to feed. Where was I? There was glass everywhere, surrounding me. I pounded on it. There were humans out there. They stared at me through the glass.

I could have them. I could kill them. I could practically taste it. I pounded on it.

Something was wrong.

There was a promise. Someone—many someones had made a promise—I wasn't supposed to be like this. Ever.

But that was a thought that belonged to someone else. Not my own thoughts anymore.

A female approached. She touched the glass. *Sleep*. I didn't sleep. I needed to *feed*.

Something smelled wrong. The world tilted left. My eyes closed.

I WOKE UP ON A BED, drenched in sweat. My mother sat next to my bed, a cool cloth on my forehead. "There he is. I think his fever broke."

"That's good." My father stared down at me. "I didn't want to have to take him to the hospital."

She rolled her eyes. "Always the pragmatist. Sounds like you were having some weird dreams."

I stared hard at my mother. She looked… younger. What was it? Well, she didn't have gray hair, and the wrinkles around her eyes were gone. She weighed more, like she was slightly rounder with fewer muscles.

I rubbed my eyes. Maybe I was seeing things. And how was my father here? "Dad, you're dead."

Hated to state the obvious, but there it was.

He stared at me before he raised an eyebrow. "Wishful dreaming, Micah? You're going to school tomorrow, so don't start any nonsense. Your mother has already missed enough work because you decided to get the flu."

"Decided to get the flu? People don't decide to get the flu. You don't opt for it. And… School? I'm a grown frickin' man. I don't go to school."

My mom gasped. "Micah. Language."

It was my hands that caught my attention. They looked different, softer. Where were the calluses and the scars? The time I'd gotten gnawed on by a Werewolf had left a serious mark. What in sweet hell was going on?

I stumbled out of bed. My legs were weak. I stared at myself in the mirror. There I was. Sixteen years old, right before the cold freeze that would make time cease to move for me for hundreds of years.

"This can't be. This is a dream."

My mother rose. "Micah Lyons. Maybe you should get back in bed."

"This is a dream." I uttered it again. "Or... or a memory. Yes, I was here. This happened. It was a memory. You took care of me. The last time, before I would be dragged off to become a Warrior in a sick, twisted world. Dad's got to go soon. He's going to be late for a meeting to talk about all the recent weird deaths. See a Vampire in lock up. You're going to offer me ginger ale and an R rated movie I've seen already but you don't know about, Mom, because you're so strict I spend half my time doing things just to get away with them."

A Wolf darted through the door, growling at me, his eyes red. No, that didn't belong in this memory. That was another time. I saw that Wolf once at Isaac Icahn's house when it tried to kill me for talking to Rachel. It had been Jason.

The memories were mixing. That Wolf shouldn't be here.

I was flung from the room. I landed on the ground. In front of me stood Brynna. She was wet, tired. Alone. I reached for her, but she ran in the opposite direction. Chad and Deacon, talking in low voices, walked right through me like I wasn't even there.

"Hello," I shouted to no one. "Hello? Help me. Someone help me."

Doubleday walked out of the woods, Isaac Icahn behind her: collared, naked, and shivering, attached to a leash. "There's no help, Micah. You belong to me now. There is only... blood."

━━

I WOKE UP SCREAMING. This time I knew where I was.

The lab where Margot worked. Chad and Deacon held me down while Margot shined a light in my eyes. "They're human pupils. They're human. Can you hear me, Micah? Are you understanding what I'm saying?"

I had to swallow before I could speak. "Fuck. Yes. What's going on? I was... I was..."

Deacon let go of my arm. "A fucking Vampire. Yes, for half a day. Let go, Chad. He's in control."

My brother looked like he had aged overnight. The shiner he'd gotten from me looked ugly and puffy. He dropped my arm and then gripped the side of the table like he needed it to stay upright. He pointed at me and then grabbed the table again. "Don't do that again."

Margot dropped the light. "He's going to be fine. He wasn't under long, and he never fed. Shouldn't have the craving, I don't think. I'm guessing, but that would be a medical guess."

She had a black eye, too. "How did you save me? What happened to your face?"

"Well, I think the fact you've been feeding off Brynna when you ah, do whatever, is why you're here. You shared enough blood that her ability to change back became, temporarily, your ability to change back. And my black eye is because I told Brynna I wasn't going to try to fix you. She had other ideas."

Deacon cleared his throat. "Never seen Brynna like that. She comes across as quiet and docile."

Then they hadn't been paying close enough attention. "She's not any of those things."

"No, she's not." Margot touched her face. "She was right, as it turns out, and not afraid to use physical force to make her point. I'll recover, and I'm glad you did. She and I might have to talk after this. After she cools off. In the presence of others."

I had to see her. If she'd gotten violent, then the part of her she feared was close to the surface. She needed to see me, and suddenly, the mate pull was more than I could handle. "Where is she?"

"Her fangs descended, and she ran for the woods about an hour ago."

I jumped off the table. Unlike my dream-self filled with memories, my legs worked fine. "I have to find her. Thank you, Margot. Thank you for saving my life."

"You saved Genesis," Deacon told me. "We drove the Vampires back because of you. We owe you a huge debt."

I stopped before I grabbed my coat off a hook on the wall. "Family doesn't require thanks and that's what everyone here is. This is my home. I can't think of a better place to risk it all for. That being said, if I can avoid it, I'm never getting bit again by anyone but Brynna." I winked at Chad. "And I'm not saying any more about that."

My brother didn't smile. "You knocked me out. I was supposed to be down there with you."

"Elizabeth needed you to be up here. I'm not sorry. I'll never be sorry I stopped you from getting bit, Chad. Hate me if you want to. I was right."

He narrowed his gaze. "You do sound like him, sometimes. Just so you know."

I didn't have to question who he meant. He was right. Deep inside of me, there would always be a little Dad.

Chapter 16

A slight dusting of snow fell on me as I made my way to Brynna. I knew exactly where she was, and I couldn't have explained why, exactly. Margot said I'd be okay because I hadn't fed, but I had... on the Vampire that made me a Vampire. I didn't know what the ramifications meant yet, and it wasn't with Margot I wanted to discover those truths.

No, it was with the woman that was mine. She stood in the wind, the gust of snow flowing around her like ice crystals. Was time moving slightly slower? I couldn't tell.

She turned to look at me, and her shoulders sagged. "I thought maybe your scent was in my mind. But you're really here. Are you okay?"

Brynna moved fast; she was in front of me as I blinked. No, things hadn't slowed. They'd sped up. Or maybe time didn't matter at all.

She was with me. We were both alive. "You hit Margot."

"I did. I'm not sorry. Arguing with me with so little time to waste?"

I raised my eyebrows. "When my father was dying, you said it was too late."

She nodded, not dropping her gaze. "I can't explain it, Micah. All I can say is I knew in my bones you could be saved, the way I know there are a few out there that can be. Margot thinks it's because you drank some of my blood."

I smirked. "I knew you'd be good for me, Brynna."

She touched my coat. "You have to be freezing. Why is this open? Why aren't you shivering?"

"I'm not feeling the cold much right now."

My love gasped. "Micah…"

"There were bound to be changes, right? We'll see what they are or if they'll go away. Maybe they will. Maybe they won't. I don't care right now." I really didn't. "I found you because of whatever changes took place. Now I want to get you out of this snow and alone in my tent."

Her eyebrows rose slowly. "Well." She smiled, a truly vixen look. "I've heard you're sort of good at that, at whatever goes on in the bedroom."

She was teasing me? "I've been told I have a certain skill set I'd be happy to continue improving for the rest of my life. But only with you."

Tears pooled in her eyes. "Your life ended yesterday, Micah. Whatever is happening now started a new one."

I pressed my thumb over her bottom lip. "That's happened to me a few times. The first time was when they shoved me in a tube and put me in cold storage. Then, the next time, was when I found out most of my newest memories were false and I came to live above ground again. Then the third time was when I met you."

She sighed. "Because I mated you."

"No." I pressed our foreheads together. I needed her, to feel her. "Not because of that. Because you made me alive again. I hadn't realized I'd died inside, but I had. Brynna, you saved me."

She kissed me, hard. It was all the encouragement I needed. I was many things but capable of making love in the snow didn't seem to be one of my skill sets, so I grabbed her hand and walked quickly toward our tent.

"Margot said you needed to feed. What were you going to do?"

She sighed. "Go down into the Vampire holding and find someone. I wouldn't have killed them. The idea made me sick to my stomach, but I would have done it."

"You feed on me."

Half of her mouth went up in a quick sort of smile. "Yes, Micah. You were healing when I needed to feed. I couldn't, you know, do that just then."

I pulled her into our tent and zipped it behind her. "I don't want to talk right now. I want to make love to you and then hold you in my arms until the morning. And then for, say, the rest of our lives."

She lay down on the bed, which must have meant she liked the idea. I started by unzipping her coat and discarding it. My body was warm, hot even, and all I wanted was inside of her. But I wouldn't rush this. Tonight felt like the first days of the rest of our lives, like we had come to this spot and I'd always know from this moment on my life would consist of before and after now.

I straddled her body as I undressed her. It took a little maneuvering, but neither of us seemed hurried. She was calm in how she tugged at my clothes and gentle when she took them off of me. I viewed her with brand new eyes. I'd worried about not being who she needed in Before Time.

That was nonsense. This was my woman. I'd always have been whatever she needed. Our souls were linked. We'd followed each other through Vampirism and cryogenic sleep until this moment. I believed. In my soul, I could feel it.

We kissed, caressing each other's lips, and I drowned happily in her sighs. This was how I wanted her. Relaxed and ready for me. I stroked my finger down her face, over the bridge of her nose, to her mouth. She bit down on my fingernail and then grinned at me.

"I love you, Micah. Please don't die again. I don't think I can take it."

I shook my head. "None of the dark right now. I love you, too."

The slowness faded. I needed her. Right then and forever. Totally naked, we pressed our bodies together in the way two people do when they understand each other's wants and needs. I knew there was a place behind her knee; if I stroked it, she would sigh. She knew I loved it when she kissed me on my chest.

We were all hands and mouths. Touching. Tasting. Loving. When I finally pressed inside of her, we both had tears in our eyes that I knew we'd never talk about. Life didn't have room for them, but in here, at this moment, they were precious sentiments of how we felt about each other. I didn't want to rush this, but the second I was deep within her warmth, all I wanted to do was lose myself within her. She wrapped her arms around my neck.

I pressed in and pulled out, lost in her noises, as though nothing outside ever existed. I pushed her knee back to get further inside of her, and she moaned loudly. "Micah. Yes. Please. More."

I'd always give her more.

And that didn't even frighten me. Not at all.

Always.

We kissed our way to completion, and when I did find home that night in between her legs, I didn't feel like a man who had died the day before and become, temporarily, a Vampire. I was the lucky asshole who got to love Brynna.

———

AS THE NEXT few days passed in a flurry of snowflakes, I started to feel the cold again. Coming back to life from the Vampire virus hadn't changed me permanently. Brynna ran a hand down my arm. "We don't have to do this."

"We do."

When I'd met Brynna, she'd had one goal in mind: find others like her who could be brought back. We were going to find them, and we were going to start the process today. The council had voted. They liked my idea of changing the setup of Genesis. They were going to have the engineers build the walls and forts.

I hoped I wasn't a total idiot and I didn't get us all killed.

Deacon tugged his coat up further. "If I get turned into a Vampire, I want your girlfriend to punch Margot."

I side-eyed him. "I'll let her know. But don't get killed. Lydia is scary. I don't want her to hurt me." I wasn't kidding. The longer I knew Lydia, the more I understood Deacon's wife would do anything for Deacon, whatever was required.

Brynna and Chad stood a little bit away from us. She turned to stare at me, and when she caught my eye, she nodded toward the group of Vampires up ahead. We were lucky. This grouping was outside. We didn't have to crawl through holes to find them. They'd been spotted, and we'd come to see if any of them set off a trigger inside Brynna.

It looked like one had.

We didn't know if this Vampire was on Margot's list of

potential Vampires who could change back or not. We'd grab the potential Vampire and go from there.

Of course, grabbing a Vampire was fine in theory, but doing it was entirely different.

"Hey." I nudged Deacon. "Glen any closer?"

"No." Deacon shook his head. "There are all kinds of things built into that small machine that are making it impossible to shut it down. Like, did you know they have somehow hooked what little electricity we do have into that thing? He could bring down the grid."

Well, that was interesting. We wouldn't be getting rid of cloning so fast, it would seem. "Do you know what he means when he says grid?"

Deacon smirked. "Fuck you. I don't."

"I didn't think so." I smiled.

He held up the device in his hand. "But he did make this while he stressed over that. It'll knock the Vampire stunned for a few minutes while we grab it."

"You zap. I grab. Chad stays here and pulls us out if we're in trouble, and Brynna tells us which one."

My best friend nodded. "Do you remember when we used to, you know, just kill them?"

"Easy days, my friend. Easy days. Ready? Brynna, which one?"

I was running the second she told me. Some things would never change. I would always love a good fight. I would always be a little crazy.

I found the right woman who got my level of nuts. And maybe she tempered it a little bit. Or maybe we were good together. Stake in hand, I'd take out any of the others who got in my way.

And because of Brynna I knew that would be a huge relief to them. We'd all been harmed in a sick game not of our doing. We had to live in it. One way or another.

As it turned out, his name was Benjamin Haynes. He lived for ten minutes after Margot returned him to his human state. Enough time for him to thank us, enough time for all of us to realize none of this would be easy. Why Brynna had lived—and why I did—was still unknown. My love wept for two days after his death. She'd held on so tightly to the idea she wasn't alone in the universe. And maybe she wasn't, but it wouldn't be Ben who would change things for Brynna.

When she could smile again, I proposed.

She wasn't alone. She'd always have me.

<hr />

TEN YEARS LATER

"WHAT DID DEACON SAY?" Brynna approached my perch on top of the outpost. I felt her coming more than witnessed it. Some things hadn't ever returned to normal after my Vampirism. Or maybe it was the mating. But my connection to my wife was super strong. I could always tell when she was near. It was like something inside of me that went cold whenever she wasn't with me warmed when she returned.

I stared out into the dark night. We weren't alone. The First Vampires were coming. I could feel it, and not because Icahn had set me up to do so. I knew they were there because the last decade had made me a hunter.

I sought them out. I killed them. The Warriors fought the regular Vampires, and I took down the big bads we hadn't even known would be our biggest problem until...

I shook my head. I didn't need to think about what happened when the First Vampires originally came right now. Brynna was here. I extended my hand, and she took it.

I drew her into me, and finally, she spoke. "Deacon says you have to deal with the crew you have. He's not making inappropriate Warriors to fill ranks."

I groaned. "The boy needs to come out here and fight for a couple of weeks. Remember what this is like."

"He would if you invited him. The last time he came out here, you told him to go back home to his wife and sons."

I had. Genesis was safe, and it always would be as long as I ran the night. The night had become my daytime. I controlled it. Here, I was in charge. "Hold on, love."

I stepped forward, pulling my bow and arrow from my back. We'd not had these special ones when Keith trained us. We hadn't known we needed them. But my brother-in-law invented and invented. I loved him for it. I'd sent Deacon back. Chad back. Rachel back. I'd sent every one of my contemporaries back home when they came because this was the life I'd promised them. I took care of the danger, and they created a universe without it inside the barriers I made for them.

This was *my* role.

Glen had invented a stake on the end of the arrow. I examined it to make sure everything was fine before I lined it up on the bow. The extra weight made balancing the bow tricky for the newbies, but during their two years with me, the newbie Warriors learned quickly. I sent the arrow into the air straight toward the First I'd been feeling. It tumbled backward, turned to dust on the ground.

Brynna sighed. "I didn't feel him."

She didn't share memories with the ones Icahn and Doubleday had created so long ago to be soldiers in a war that would never happen. They'd messed with the genome, created a virus they'd never really understand, and we all lived with it now.

"That's okay. I did."

We stared into the night together, and she finally pulled back to stare at my face. "If Deacon won't play ball, you know what has to happen."

"Can we get a note to Jason? He'll reach out to the Werewolves. Margot will be on board. She can make it okay with the council after the fact. I'll make apologies, instead of asking permission."

Brynna nodded. "We can, and she will. This will end it. We're almost to a point where it's okay out there, Micah. I can see a future where we win."

She'd become an optimist, and I loved her for it. I wasn't. I never would be. That was okay. I was the man I had to be. As long as she loved me, I was enough. As long as she loved me, *we* were enough.

I DON'T KNOW if anyone will ever read this. If I get to live to be an old man, I'm just going to be that crazy man in the Outpost the kids talk about because he's muttering to himself or something. But my sister-in-law said to write this up, and so I did. My wife is calling to me. Got to go.

Other books by Rebecca Royce...

Wings of Artemis

Kidnapped By Her Husbands

Rescued by Their Wife

Crashing Into Destiny

Meeting Them

Reclaiming Their Love

Loving Them

Ship Called Malice

Saving Them

Dark Demise

Light Unfolding (coming soon)

Last Hope

Tradition Be Damned

Past Be Damned

Destiny Be Damned

Compassion Be Damned (coming soon)

Dragon Wars

Forever

Eternal

Always

Evermore

Endless

Wards and Wands
Hexed and Vexed
Curse Reversed (coming soon)

Safe Haven
Everywhere and Nowhere
Dimension X (coming soon)
More coming soon....

Soul Bound
Prisoner of the Dragons
More coming soon....

Shadow Promised
Strange Days
Weird Nights
Bizarre Years
More coming soon...

The Warrior
Initiation
Driven
Subversive
Redemption
Justice

Warrior World (spin off of The Warrior)

Deacon

Micah (coming soon)

The Westervelt Wolves

Her Wolf

Summer's Wolf

Wolf Reborn

Wolf's Valentine

Wolf's Magic

Alpha Wolf

Angel's Wolf

Darkest Wolf

Lone Wolf

Fallen Alpha

Alpha Rising

Alpha's Strength

Alpha's Sacrifice

Alpha's Truth

Alpha Enticing

Hidden Alpha (coming soon)

The Capes

Seductive Powers

Adrenaline Rush

Last Ascension

The Conditioned

Eye Contact

Embraced

Unlawful (coming soon…)

The Outsiders

Love Beyond Time

Love Beyond Sanity

Love Beyond Loyalty

Love Beyond Sight

Love Beyond Expectations

Love Beyond Oceans

Love Beyond Flames

Love Beyond Lies (coming soon)

Cascade

Haunted Redemption

Phoenix Everlasting

Fragility Unearthed

Persuasion Enraptured

Reverse Harem Story

Unconventional

Unexpected (coming soon)

Stand Alone Titles

Planet Bear